# Cul-de-Sac Kids

## Collection Three

# BOOKS BY BEVERLY LEWIS

## Picture Books

*Annika's Secret Wish*
*In Jesse's Shoes*
*Just Like Mama*
*What Is God Like?*
*What Is Heaven Like?*

## Children's Fiction

### CUL-DE-SAC KIDS°

*Cul-de-Sac Kids Collection One*
*Cul-de-Sac Kids Collection Two*
*Cul-de-Sac Kids Collection Three*
*Cul-de-Sac Kids Collection Four*

## Youth Fiction

### GIRLS ONLY (GO!)*

*Girls Only! Volume One*
*Girls Only! Volume Two*

### SUMMERHILL SECRETS+

*SummerHill Secrets Volume One*
*SummerHill Secrets Volume Two*

### HOLLY'S HEART+

*Holly's Heart Collection One*
*Holly's Heart Collection Two*
*Holly's Heart Collection Three*

*www.beverlylewis.com*

* 4 books in each volume   + 5 books in each volume   ° 6 books in each volume

# Cul-de-Sac Kids
## Collection Three

BOOKS 13–18

# Beverly Lewis

BETHANYHOUSE
a division of Baker Publishing Group
Minneapolis, Minnesota

© 1997, 1998 by Beverly Lewis

Previously published in six separate volumes:
  *Tarantula Toes* © 1997
  *Green Gravy* © 1997
  *Backyard Bandit Mystery* © 1997
  *Tree House Trouble* © 1998
  *The Creepy Sleep-Over* © 1998
  *The Great TV Turn-Off* © 1998

Published by Bethany House Publishers
11400 Hampshire Avenue South
Bloomington, Minnesota 55438
www.bethanyhouse.com

Bethany House Publishers is a division of
Baker Publishing Group, Grand Rapids, Michigan

Printed in the United States of America

ISBN 978-0-7642-3050-9

Library of Congress Control Number: 2017945876

These stories are works of fiction. Names, characters, incidents, and dialogues
are products of the author's imagination and are not to be construed as real.
Any resemblance to any person, living or dead, is purely coincidental.

Cover design by Eric Walljasper
Cover illustration by Paul Turnbaugh
Story illustrations by Janet Huntington

18  19  20  21  22  23  24      7  6  5  4  3  2  1

# Contents

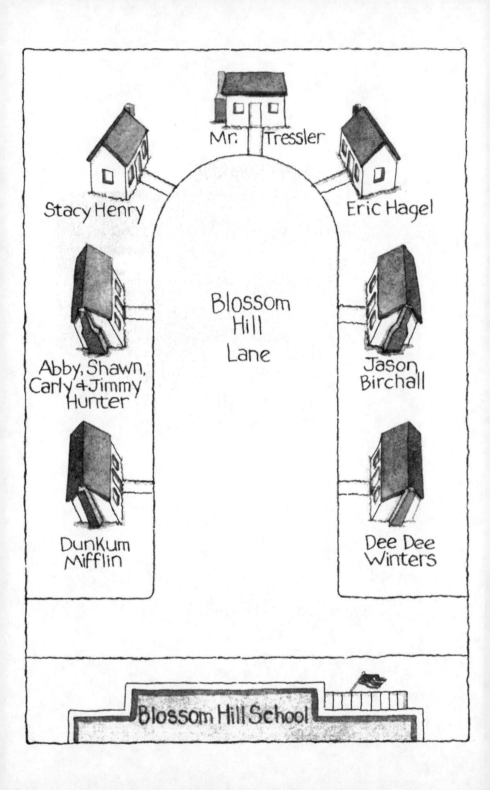

# BOOK 13

# Tarantula Toes

To
three of my young fans,
all in one family!

Chris, Collin, and Linsi Stoddard

# One

Jason Birchall zipped through his homework.

*I have to tell someone my secret!* he thought.

He didn't bother to check his spelling. He
didn't even read over his work.

Jason was in such a big hurry. He slapped
his name on the paper and pushed his homework into a folder.

Then he dashed outside.

It was still light, so he jumped on his bike.

His friends Dunkum and Eric were already out riding. They zoomed up Blossom
Hill Lane when they saw him. "Hey, Jason!"
they called. "Wanna ride?"

"You bet!" Jason said.

"Did you finish your homework already?"

Dunkum asked. His real name was Edward Mifflin. And he was always talking school stuff.

"Yahoo! It's done," Jason hollered. "But let's not talk about that."

He glanced around.

Was it safe?

He made his voice sound mysterious. "Listen up, guys."

Eric stared at Jason. "Why are you talking like that?" Eric said.

"Because," said Jason.

"Because why?" Dunkum asked.

"Because I've got a secret," Jason said.

"So tell us," Eric said. "I'm sure you're dying to."

Jason smiled. His friends knew him well. "OK, I'll tell you. But you have to promise not to say one word to the girls."

Dunkum's face lit up. "You can trust us. You know that."

Eric agreed. "We promise."

Jason looked over his shoulder. "Are we really alone?"

Dunkum nodded. "It's just us guys."

"Let's not take any chances," Jason said.

He motioned to Eric and Dunkum, and the three of them headed up the driveway. When they reached the garage door, Jason whispered, "I'm starting a zoo."

"*That's* your secret?" Dunkum said.

"Shh!" Jason peered around, checking for the other Cul-de-Sac Kids. "It's top secret."

"Are we talking a real zoo?" Eric asked.

Jason leaned a little closer. "You heard right. June is Zoo Month, so I'm starting a REAL zoo in my room."

Eric scratched his head. "Does your mom know about this?"

"My parents think it'll be an adventure."

"You mean like a learning experience?" Dunkum said with a frown.

"That's exactly right." Jason reached into his pocket. He unfolded a page out of the newspaper.

Eric leaned on his bike for a closer look. "Whatcha got?"

"Check out my super secret," Jason said. He pointed to a picture of a big, hairy spider. "I'm gonna buy *this*."

Eric gulped. "Is that what I think it is?"

"It's a tarantula, all right," Jason said proudly.

"Hey, let me see." Dunkum grabbed the paper. "Whoa! I can almost see Abby Hunter's hair sticking straight up!"

Abby was the president of the Cul-de-Sac Kids. Nine kids on one block. A really cool club.

Jason started jumping around. "Stacy Henry will freak out, too. So will Dee Dee and Carly!"

"Wow, what a scary spider!" Eric said. "Are you buying him just to scare the girls?"

"Shh! How can you say that?" Jason said. But he didn't stop grinning or hopping. He felt good all over. "It's a pinktoe tarantula, and he's gonna be all mine!"

"I don't know about this," Dunkum said. He studied the picture a little longer. "A tarantula might not be such a good idea."

Jason pushed up his glasses. "What do you mean?"

"They eat frogs, right?" asked Dunkum.

Jason started to laugh. "Oh, I get it! You're thinking about Croaker. But you shouldn't be. My new pet will *not* be eating frogs."

Jason knew exactly what to feed Pinktoes. His spider book told all about tarantulas. Everything he needed to know. There was even a chapter on how to handle spiders.

"Crickets and earthworms are Pinktoe's favorite snacks," Jason spoke up.

"Well, good luck finding insects like that around here," Dunkum said. He handed the newspaper back.

Jason looked at Dunkum. His friend was probably right. Crickets needed plenty of oxygen. The air was thin in this part of Colorado.

"Don't worry," Jason said. "I'll take good care of Pinktoes. You'll see. I might even let him crawl on me."

Dunkum's eyes were big and black now. Really black. "What about fangs?" he asked. "Don't tarantulas bite?"

"*I'm* not afraid," Jason bragged.

Eric looked a little pale.

Dunkum looked worried.

"I'll have Pinktoes by tomorrow," Jason said. "Then you'll see how brave I am."

"Tomorrow? That soon?" Eric said.

Before Jason could answer, Eric hopped on his bike and rode away.

Dunkum did, too.

Jason wasn't surprised. Some kids were just fraidycats. But not him. He was going to be the bravest kid in the world.

Besides, no one else had a zoo in his bedroom.

No one else had a pinktoe tarantula all the way from South America.

Not a single Cul-de-Sac Kid!

*I'll be the only tarantula keeper around,* he thought.

He could hardly wait.

# Two

At last, it was Saturday.

Tarantula time!

Jason awoke early, even before his parents.

Rolling over, he found the newspaper ad. Right where he'd left it—under his pillow!

He burst out laughing. Dunkum and Eric would shake with fear. They'd shiver and shake if they knew. He was sure they would.

Whoever slept on a picture of spiders?

A kid with courage. That's who!

Just then, his father called to him. "What's so funny over there?"

His dad was up. *Yes!*

Jason rushed into the hallway. He stood at his parents' bedroom door. "Ready for a visit to the pet store?" he asked.

His mother made funny little noises. She sounded half asleep.

The door opened.

Mr. Birchall was wearing a bathrobe. "You're awake too early, son," he said.

Jason pushed his glasses up. "Because I can't wait. Let's go get my spider!"

His father smiled and headed for the kitchen.

Jason was right on his heels. "C'mon, let's go *now!*"

"Are you really sure about this spider purchase?" Dad asked. "Have you thought it through?"

Jason couldn't believe his ears.

"Of course I'm sure," he said. "The tank's all set up. Everything's ready."

"And you followed all the directions?"

Jason nodded. "I followed everything exactly right."

Dad smiled. "And you'll be very careful if you decide to handle your new pet?"

"*If* I do? I *know* I will!"

His father put a firm hand on Jason's shoulder. "You must be gentle, son. Tarantulas are delicate pets."

"I'll be the best spider keeper ever," Jason promised. "You'll see."

■ ■ ■

In a hurry, Jason got dressed for the day. He heard his dad humming in the shower.

Bacon-and-egg smells floated from the kitchen.

"Today's tarantula day," he told his mother.

"What a brave one you are," she said. "I don't know how you even look at those spiders. And to think one of those hairy things is coming to live in my house."

"Pinktoes will live in *my* bedroom," Jason reminded her. "He'll stay in his tank . . . most of the time."

Mrs. Birchall's hand flew to her throat. "Most of the time? Don't you mean *all* of the time?"

"Oh, not when I'm showing him off," Jason explained. "Sometimes, he'll be on display."

His mother's eyebrows arched. "Oh?"

"There's nothing to worry about. Nothing at all."

"I hope not." She wiped her forehead. "I really do."

At breakfast, Jason and his parents talked all about the spider.

"He needs cork bark to climb on," Jason said.

"We'll buy some today," Dad said. "Crickets too."

"I'll dig for earthworms after lunch," Jason suggested. "A tasty treat for a tarantula."

"Good thinking," Mother said. She wrinkled up her nose. The subject of worms was a no-no at the table.

"Uh . . . sorry, Mom," Jason said.

"It would be much better if we talked *after* we eat," she said.

A wink came from Jason's father.

And Jason understood.

But gross stuff didn't bother him. Not one bit. Worms or crickets, spiders and frogs were just fine.

Any old time!

# Three

The ride downtown took forever.

*Faster. Hurry . . . hurry,* thought Jason.

Even the light stayed red too long.

Jitter, jitter. Jump, jerk. Jason couldn't sit still.

"Excited?" asked his dad.

"Pinktoes comes home today!" Jason said. Then he spied the pet shop sign.

His father parked the car. "Have you told your friends yet?" he asked.

"I told only two."

"The boys?" His father was grinning.

"I told Dunkum and Eric. They promised not to tell it around," Jason explained.

"So it's a secret?"

"A super spider secret!" Jason said. He leaped out of the car and raced to the pet store.

Inside, a large glass tank was waiting. A tiny tan spider was perched in the corner.

Pinktoes was nowhere to be seen.

"Where's my spider?" Jason wailed.

The clerk hurried over. "May I help you?"

"Where's Pinktoes?"

"Wait one moment," said the clerk.

Jason took off his glasses and twirled them on his finger. He jittered and jived.

"Someone bought my spider," he fussed. "Bought him out from under my nose!"

His father shook his head. "Don't worry, son. Here comes the store owner."

A tall man smiled at them. "We're getting more pinktoe tarantulas in on Monday."

"*Two* more days? That's way too long," Jason said.

"Sorry about the wait," the man said. "I'll be happy to put your name on one."

"*My* name?" Jason looked at his dad.

"He means he'll save one for you," his father explained.

"Oh . . . sure, that would be great!" Jason burst out.

But he didn't feel great inside.

Dunkum and Eric would never believe

this. They'd think he was fooling about getting a super spider. They'd say he was making it all up.

"We'll be back on Monday," Jason's father said.

"Right after school," added Jason. "And not a minute later!"

His father nodded.

The pet store owner waved.

And Jason shuffled his feet to the car.

■■■

The ride home went too fast.

All green lights.

*Phooey.*

Jason scooted down in the front seat. He didn't want Dunkum and Eric to see him. Not without Pinktoes.

*How will I tell them?* he thought.

Then he had an idea. He'd say that Pinktoes was crawling home. He'd say that the tarantula was last seen headed this way. A big black tarantula was on the loose. Headed for Blossom Hill Lane!

That's what Jason decided.

It was a whopping lie.

But Dunkum and Eric would be scared silly.

# Four

The car was hardly in the driveway. But here came Dunkum and Eric, running. *Rats!* thought Jason.

Dunkum called to him from behind a tree. "Where's your big, mean spider?" he asked.

Jason glanced over at his dad. He didn't want him to hear what he was going to say.

"Hello, boys," his dad said, waving at Dunkum and Eric. Then he went inside the house.

Jason got out of the car. He stood tall. Now he could tell his made-up story.

"I thought you were buying a hairy monster," Dunkum said. "Where is it?"

The boys stayed close to the tree.

"And *I* thought you were too scared to see him," Jason replied.

"Well, we're not," Eric said. "We're braver than you think."

Jason lowered his voice. "If you really wanna know, he's on the loose. And coming this way!"

Eric looked around. "I don't see anything."

"You just wait," Jason said. But he felt funny inside.

Dunkum scratched his head. He inched close. "You mean your pet spider is crawling here? To Blossom Hill Lane?"

It sounded very fishy. Foolish too.

Jason almost laughed at his own words. But he pulled himself together. "You heard me," he said. "Pinktoes is on the prowl. He's coming. You'd better watch out!"

Eric was still staring at the ground, looking for super spiders. "Better share your secret and warn the girls, then," Eric said. "They won't want to see a scary spider around here."

"No!" Jason shouted. "Don't tell them. We have to keep it a secret."

"How come?" Dunkum said. He was still frowning.

*He doesn't believe me*, thought Jason. *He knows I'm lying.*

"So . . . what's the expected time of arrival?" asked Dunkum. "For your tarantula, I mean."

"Oh, I don't know," Jason spoke up. "It might take him till Monday."

That part was sort of true. But not true enough.

Eric stared at him. "Can spiders smell their way? Like dogs and cats do?"

Jason swallowed hard.

*Rats.*

What could he say? More lies?

"Uh, I don't know for sure," he mumbled. "Maybe they can. But I think I hear my mother calling."

"I don't hear anything," Eric said. He looked at Dunkum.

"Me neither," Dunkum said.

Both boys gave Jason a weird look.

"Go ahead and find your mom," Dunkum said. His face had a big grin. "Eric and I will be on the lookout for your tarantula."

"Don't step on him," Jason warned. "He's part of my zoo."

Dunkum Mifflin laughed out loud. He laughed all the way down the cul-de-sac.

"Double rats!" Jason said to himself.

■■■

Jason could hardly eat lunch.

His hamburger stuck in his throat.

"What's wrong, dear?" his mother asked.

"I'm not hungry," he replied.

"Are you sick?" she asked.

*Sick of lying*, he thought. But he didn't say that.

He didn't know what to do. Dunkum and Eric would never believe him now. Not even if he tried to tell the truth.

The whole truth.

He'd just have to wait two more days.

By Monday everyone would know about Pinktoes. Especially Dunkum and Eric. Then they could see for themselves.

But Jason was worried.

What if the spider shipment didn't come? What would he tell his friends? Another made-up story?

He carried his plate to the sink.

"Sorry about your spider," his mother said.

His father spoke up. "It's supposed to arrive on Monday."

Jason shrugged.

*Supposed to*, he thought.

He felt even worse.

# Five

On Monday, math class took forever.

*Yuck times two*, thought Jason.

Science lasted too long. So did morning and afternoon recess.

*Double phooey.*

Jason didn't say much to Dunkum or Eric. And they didn't ask about Pinktoes.

*I hope they're keeping my secret*, Jason thought.

But he knew better. They weren't talking because they didn't believe him.

Not one bit.

■■■

After school, Jason waited for his father. Time to go to the pet store. Again!

This time, Jason didn't go near the glass tank.

He was a jittery worrywart. He crossed his fingers behind his back.

The clerk came right over. "Jason Birchall, right? We have a pinktoe tarantula with your name on it."

Jason couldn't help it. He smiled. "Cool stuff," he said.

The spider shipment had come!

Now Dunkum and Eric could freak out. They could be fraidycats. But best of all, they'd believe him.

Jason peeked at the glass tank. He whispered, "How's it going, Pinktoes?"

The spider was as still as the moon.

Was he breathing?

Nothing moved. Not even his fangs.

"Today you're gonna become a Cul-de-Sac Kid's pet. *My* pet," Jason explained.

The black spider started to move. His long legs crawled toward the glass. He came up to Jason's face as he looked through the glass.

"Excuse me, young man," the clerk said.

Jason stepped back.

The man removed the top on the tank.

Jason pointed to the black tarantula. "I want that one." The spider's long legs had pinkish spots on the tips.

"He's beautiful," said the clerk. "A very good choice. I hope you've read up on these furry fellows."

"Oh yes," Jason replied. "I know all about them."

"Then you know how to pick them up?" the man asked.

Jason nodded. "With my fingers away from its fangs."

"Very good." Then the man showed him how to handle the spider.

"That's how my spider book said to do it," said Jason, watching.

"OK," said the clerk. "You're all set."

*Yahoo!*

Jason felt like a billion bucks. But he only had twenty-five. Plenty to buy his new pet.

His father spoke up. "Jason knows a lot about *frogs*, too."

"Oh?" the man said. "Do you own a frog?"

"Yes, but Croaker and Pinktoes won't be tank mates," Jason was quick to say. "Besides, Pinktoes doesn't eat frogs."

The clerk's eyelids blinked. "You're one hundred percent correct."

"I *have* to be," Jason said. "It's Zoo Month. And I'm starting my very own zoo."

"A zoo?"

"A zoo in my room." Jason grinned.

"An excellent place for your Pinktoes," said the clerk. "Now, that'll be nineteen dollars."

*Flash!* Out came Jason's wallet. He'd saved up for a long time.

"Just one spider today?" asked the man.

"One for now," Jason said. "Maybe more later."

"We'll see about that," his father said. "We'll see what kind of zoo keeper you are."

Jason smiled a big smile. The best part of the day had finally come.

Pinktoes was going home.

*Hooray!*

# Six

After supper, Jason went to Dunkum's house.

"There's a super spider in the cul-de-sac," he said.

"Yeah, right." Dunkum's eyes narrowed.

"I'm *not* kidding," Jason said. "Come over and see for yourself."

Dunkum rolled his eyes. "He didn't *really* crawl all the way from the pet store. Did he?"

Jason shook his head. "I should've told you the truth before. I'm sorry."

"Why'd you lie?"

Jason shrugged his shoulders. "I thought you'd laugh at me. I thought—"

"Forget it," Dunkum said. "Just don't do it again. Deal?"

"Double deal." Jason started to feel better inside. "When do you wanna see Pinktoes?" he asked.

"Maybe after school tomorrow," Dunkum said, but he looked like he didn't believe Jason.

"OK, see you then." Jason ran next door to Abby Hunter's house.

He invited her and Carly, her little sister, over. And their adopted Korean brothers, Shawn and Jimmy.

"Yikes, I don't know," Abby said. "Sounds creepy. Do you *really* have a tarantula?"

Jason grinned. "Sure do! And Pinktoes will stay in his tank. Don't worry."

Carly and Jimmy came to the door.

"Wanna go see Jason's tarantula?" Abby asked them. "He says it's from South America."

Jimmy frowned. "Spider no get here from there." He was still learning to speak English.

Carly took two steps back. "A tarantula? Nobody has a pet like *that*!" Her eyes were wide and round.

Jason stood tall. "I should warn you, he looks very scary."

"Well, Carly and I probably won't come, then," Abby said.

"Jimmy not think there is big spider!" shouted Jimmy. "No way."

Jason scratched his head. "Well, it's true. Better come tomorrow and see for yourself."

Next, he went to Stacy Henry's house.

"No, thanks," she said. "I *hate* spiders!"

"Too bad for you," he said.

Jason crossed the street.

Eric Hagel would be dying to see Pinktoes. Jason was sure of it. Eric would be scared silly, but he'd come anyway.

Jason was right about his friend.

"Promise to leave your spider in the tank?" Eric said. "If you *really* own a pinktoes."

"I really do," Jason said. "And I'll keep him in the tank."

Next he headed for Dee Dee Winter's house.

She was playing outside with her crabby cat, Mister Whiskers.

"Wanna come see my tarantula?" Jason asked.

*"Ee-yew!"* Dee Dee screamed. "Get away

from me, Jason Birchall! Don't make up scary lies!"

"Sorry I stopped by," Jason muttered.

He pulled himself together and marched home.

# Seven

It was Tuesday.

Miss Hershey was writing on the board. Her back was to the class.

*Perfect!*

Jason glanced at Abby Hunter.

When she looked at him, he made his fingers wiggle and crawl. Just like a spider. A big one.

Abby shook her head and frowned at him.

*Line leader*, Miss Hershey wrote. *Stacy Henry*.

Stacy grinned, probably because line leader was her favorite job.

"Lucky Stacy," someone whispered.

Jason stared at Stacy. Then he made a wriggling spider with his hand.

Stacy's eyebrows floated up. She looked the other way.

Miss Hershey wrote on the board: *Hamster helper—Jason Birchall.*

Jason sat tall. *Yahoo!*

Feeding the hamster was the best job. The coolest for a zoo keeper. A zoo-in-his-room keeper!

The class said the pledge.

"I pledge allegiance to the flag," Jason began. But he was thinking about his tarantula.

He couldn't stop thinking about Pinktoes. He thought so hard, he missed six spelling words. He thought so long, he forgot to feed the hamster.

"What is wrong today?" Shawn Hunter asked at recess.

"Nothing," Jason said. "Are you coming to my house after school?"

"To see fake spider?"

"Didn't Abby tell you?" Jason asked.

"Abby not tell me. Little brother tell about pretend spider." Shawn's eyes nearly closed shut.

"So . . . are you coming?" asked Jason.

"I not believe you," Shawn said.

Jason shrugged. Nobody did.

He was the bravest tarantula owner around. And no one believed him!

Then he and Shawn ran to the soccer field.

■■■

After school, Jason stood on his front porch.

He wondered if maybe, just maybe, someone would show up. The sun was in his eyes, so he sat on the step.

*Why don't my friends believe me?* he thought.

Across the street, Carly and Dee Dee were cutting out paper dolls.

Abby and Stacy were walking their dogs.

The boys were nowhere to be seen.

Jason waited and waited. He went inside to check the clock.

Next, he went to his room.

Everything was set.

Croaker seemed well behaved. He sat quietly in his glass home on the dresser. He blinked his eyes at Jason.

Pinktoes was in his tank on the bookcase. He flicked his fangs.

The zoo room was absolutely perfect.

Jason tiptoed to Pinktoe's tank. "I think everyone's a fraidycat," he said. "Everyone on Blossom Hill Lane!"

Pinktoes looked like he was snoozing. He didn't budge a single black hair. He was probably dreaming about his next cricket.

Jason went to the living room. He sat on the sofa.

He stayed there till supper.

But no one showed up. Not a single brave kid.

"It's very quiet around here," his mother said.

Jason got up and helped to set the table.

"I was sorta expecting company," he said. "But no one came."

"That's strange," she said. "Don't the Cul-de-Sac Kids stick together?"

"What?" Jason said.

His mother repeated the familiar words.

*That's it*, Jason thought. *They're sticking together! They think I'm lying . . . again.*

He felt foolish. And very upset.

Just then an idea hit him.

"I'll show them I'm not lying," he whispered to himself. "I'll take Pinktoes' picture!"

He was going to prove himself.

The Cul-de-Sac Kids would have to believe him now.

Then he had another idea.

It was a better-than-good idea.

He would have a spider show. He'd invite all the kids. They could see the picture, then come to his amazing show.

*Yahoo!*

# Eight

After supper, Jason took a bunch of pictures. He used his dad's digital camera. Then he printed the pictures and made invitations. Eight in all. One for every Cul-de-Sac Kid, not counting himself.

He drew a big black spider on the front, then wrote the message.

Jason licked each envelope shut.

He thought of all the money he would make. What a cool idea.

Eight kids times seventy-five cents. Six whole bucks!

Six dollars would buy a lot of crickets.

If only he could get the kids to come.

He could hear Dunkum bouncing his basketball at the first house. He stuck the

Come see
Jason Birchall,
Taractula Tamer!!!
Featuring a Sothuth American
Super Spider, Pink Toes!!
(fierce fangs, venom, and ALL!!!)
When? Thursday after school
Where? Jason's front yard
How much? 75 Cents per kid

invitation and the picture of Pinktoes on the front door.

Dunkum glanced his way. "Whatcha got?"

"Something for you." Jason forced a smile.

"Oh . . . thanks," Dunkum said. But he was frowning again.

"You didn't show up today," Jason said.

Dunkum shot a basket. "I know."

"Well, I thought we had a deal. You know, about not lying?" Jason said.

"I never promised to come."

"Did too," Jason said.

Dunkum shook his head. "I said maybe."

Jason shook his head. He wasn't going to push for answers. He'd let the invitation and the picture do their jobs.

"Well . . . see you," Jason said. And he left.

At Abby's house, he stuffed four invitations in the screen door. One for each Hunter kid.

Then he went around the block and delivered the rest.

He almost stopped to visit Mr. Tressler. He was the old man at the end of the cul-de-sac.

But Jason was too busy. He had some practicing to do. Lots of it.

The Brave Tarantula Tamer had a cool super spider. But no amazing act to go with it.

So he hurried home.

First things first. He needed a pair of thin rubber gloves. Something to protect his hands.

He borrowed his mother's kitchen gloves. They were too big, but better than nothing.

Jason dashed to his bedroom. "OK, Pinktoes, it's you and me," he said.

Gently, he took off the lid and reached inside.

Very slowly, the tarantula crawled onto his gloved hand.

"Nice and easy," he whispered.

He had a jumpy stomach. But he had to be brave.

Pinktoes mustn't sense his fear. Not now. Not for their first time together.

"Here you go," he said softly.

Jason put his left hand next to his right. He held them close together. That way, Pinktoes wouldn't fall.

He must *not* fall, because his body was very delicate. Falling could be a deadly thing.

Pinktoes went from one hand to the other.

Under the gloves, Jason got goose pimples on his goose bumps.

"Cool stuff," he said, but not too loudly. He didn't want to scare his new zoo friend.

"Can you do it again?" he asked.

Jason moved his hand back. He held his breath.

The tarantula kept going.

"Good for you," Jason said.

He didn't want to tire Pinktoes out. So he put him back in the glass tank.

"We'll practice again tomorrow. OK?"

Pinktoes did not reply, but that was fine. *Anyone knows tarantulas don't talk.*

Still, Jason waited. He watched his spider climb the cork bark. "We're having a show in two days," he whispered.

Could he pull it off?

Jason tried not to worry. He looked out his bedroom window.

The Hunter kids—Abby, Carly, Shawn, and Jimmy—sat on their front steps. They were looking at his invitations. And the pictures.

*Will they come?* he wondered.

Silently, he closed the curtains.

He crossed his fingers and hoped so.

# Nine

The next morning, Jason got up before the sun.

He pulled on his mother's kitchen gloves. Time to practice his spider act again.

Today, he was more sure of himself. Much more.

And things went very well.

Jason decided he was braver now. He would practice without the gloves after breakfast.

His mother wasn't told about it. Nope.

*This* was top secret.

Jason made his hands flat and firm, and Pinktoes crawled over them.

It tickled just a little. But Jason felt comfortable with his pet.

No gloves. And no bites.

*Perfect.*

"We'll practice again right after school," he said.

And off he went to school, feeling braver than ever.

■■■

During recess, he had an idea. It was kinda crazy.

He watched Jimmy Hunter playing in the sandpit. Jimmy was barefoot.

That's when the idea hit.

*Could Pinktoes walk over my bare toes?* Jason thought.

He laughed out loud and couldn't wait to find out.

"What's so funny?" a small voice said.

Jason spun around.

It was Dee Dee Winters.

"Oh, hi," he said.

"Why are you laughing?" she asked. "I don't see anything funny."

"Oh, it's nothing," Jason said.

Dee Dee made her face twist up. "Well, I don't know about that, Jason Birchall. Laughing over nothing is pretty weird."

He stood as tall as he could. "Oh, you'll see."

"See what?"

"You'll see what's so funny if you come to my show. If you're *brave* enough."

"Come to a silly spider show? Why would I wanna do that?" Dee Dee giggled.

Jason hated it when she giggled. But he kept smiling. "Because it's gonna be amazing. I'm gonna handle my tarantula with *bare hands!*" he replied. "That's why you should come."

"Really?" Her eyes were bright now.

"Oh, it'll be so thrilling. Creepy, crawly stuff. Fangs and venom—you know, spider stuff. Better come and see." Jason grinned.

Surely this would get her attention.

The other Cul-de-Sac Kids would probably hear about it, too.

Dee Dee was a little girl with a big mouth. She would spread the word.

Jason was counting on it.

# Ten

**T**hursday afternoon came quickly.

*All* the Cul-de-Sac Kids were gathered in Jason's front yard.

He couldn't believe his eyes.

*Good work, Dee Dee*, he thought. Her blabby mouth had worked wonders.

"This is super great," he told Pinktoes. "They've come for the show."

He carried the glass tank out to the front porch. Carefully, he set it down.

Then he turned to greet his friends. "Welcome to the most amazing spider show on earth!"

He wished he had a trio of trumpets. He could hear them in his head. *Tah-dah-dah-dah!*

"Everyone sit on the grass," he said. "Make yourselves comfortable."

He was having a double dabble good time. That's what Abby always liked to say.

Dee Dee and Carly seemed nervous, though. Abby would call them jitterbugs for sure.

Abby and her best friend, Stacy Henry, were standing nearby, eyes wide.

Dunkum and Eric sat cross-legged in the grass. Shawn and Jimmy Hunter seemed a little bit excited.

First things first.

Jason passed his baseball cap around. *Chinkle . . . chink.* The kids dropped their money inside.

Jason was laughing under his breath. They'd all come to see his daring show. A super spider show.

But there was something his friends didn't know. The best spider secret known to man. It was the *big* secret about the spider's fangs!

Jason couldn't wait to fool his friends.

"I will now pick up the tarantula," Jason announced. "Quiet, please. Pinktoes will perform best if it's quiet."

Dee Dee and Carly giggled. But they seemed edgy.

Whispers rippled through the group. Someone said something about the fangs. And the venom.

It was perfect. The kids were really scared.

"Shh!" Jason said. "I must have it quiet."

He waited for the group to settle down.

Finally, no one spoke.

He picked up his tarantula. Very carefully, he sat down in the grass.

Slowly, he passed his gloved hands back and forth.

Carly was hiding her eyes. Dee Dee was peeking.

Abby and Stacy looked absolutely frightened.

But the boys looked brave. Dunkum and Eric watched without blinking. Shawn and Jimmy smiled.

Jason was glad his friends were enjoying the show.

They didn't know his secret.

He put his spider in the glass tank. He removed the gloves. Next, he reached back in and picked up the tarantula again.

There was a chorus of *oohs*. From the girls, mostly.

Dunkum whispered, "Whoa!"

"Now I will let Pinktoes crawl on my bare hands," Jason said. "Remember, he has fangs!"

Dee Dee and Carly squeaked a little.

But nobody made another sound.

Jason held his tarantula correctly. Far away from the fangs.

He sat on the grass again. Then he crossed his legs. One bare foot stuck high in the air.

Without a sound, he set the tarantula on his toes.

Jason grinned and put his hands behind his head.

"Tah-dah!" he said. "Just call me Mister Tarantula Toes!"

Quickly, he reached to free his pet from the high perch.

But before he could, Pinktoes jumped into the air.

*Plop!*

The tarantula landed on Jason's head.

"Ee-yew!" the girls screamed.

Jason felt a stab of pain in his forehead.

"Ouch!" he hollered. "The fangs!"

# Eleven

"Jason, are you all right?" Abby asked.

The Cul-de-Sac Kids gathered around.

"Is he gonna die?" Carly asked.

"Lie still," Jason's mother said to him. She had heard all the noise and come outside. She looked at Jason's friends. "Why do you think he might die?" she asked.

Jason spoke up. He felt terrible, but not from the spider bite. "People don't die from spider venom," he mumbled.

Eric frowned. "But you said—"

"I tricked you on purpose," Jason said. "I didn't tell the truth about Pinktoes."

His mother finished treating the wound.

Soon Jason sat up and looked at each kid. "I wanted to fool you, to get back at all of you for not believing me."

"Well, you did a good job of it," Stacy said.

"He sure did!" Dee Dee said.

Jason felt the tiny lump on his forehead. "I shouldn't have made you think Pinktoes was a monster. With poison in his fangs."

"Well, he *is* scary looking," Stacy said.

"I think he's beautiful," said Jason.

"Not to me," Abby said.

Jason began to explain. "Tarantulas are gentle pets. Their bites are milder than a beesting."

"What about that nasty bump on your head?" Dee Dee pointed to the swelling. "That doesn't look so good."

"It'll go away," Jason's mother said. She helped him up. "It's nothing to worry about."

"For sure?" Carly asked.

Jason smiled and nodded. His friends cared about him. They really did.

*He* wanted to be a better friend, too. Starting right now.

"Pinktoes was terrified," Jason said. "That's the only reason he bit me. Tarantulas don't bite unless they're frightened. Or feel in danger. I never should have put him up so high."

The kids peeked inside the glass tank.

They wanted to see the jumping spider up close.

All except Dee Dee and Carly. They didn't want to look.

Dunkum and Eric inched closer to the tank. "Can we feed Pinktoes sometime?"

"Sure," Jason said. "Wanna help me dig for his supper?"

"When?" asked Shawn.

"Right now," answered Jason.

Shawn rubbed his hands together. His dark eyes twinkled.

"Remember the Mudhole Mystery?" said Jason.

"Sure do!" Dunkum said. "Ooey-gooey mud is great for worms. Worms are fun."

"Worms are *not* fun. But worms are good for spider snacks," someone said.

Jason and the boys turned around.

It was Abby. She was hiding something behind her.

"Whatcha got?" Jason asked. He tried to peek around her.

Abby stepped back. "I'll show you if you make a promise," she said.

Jason shrugged. "What kind of promise?"

"No more lies," she said.

Dunkum and Eric were laughing.

But Abby wasn't. "Well?" she said.

Jason pinched up his face. Being pushed into a corner was no fun. Especially by a girl.

"I'm waiting," she said.

Dunkum was holding his sides. He was laughing too hard.

"The club president has spoken," Eric said.

Jason teased, "But is she brave?"

Abby held out a jar of wiggly worms. "Here's proof."

"Hey, cool," said Jason. "Thanks!"

Abby put her hands on her hips. "*Now* do you promise?"

"OK, OK," Jason said. "I promise. And I mean it."

She smiled. "You can be a double dabble mischief-maker," Abby said. "But you're a good friend."

"You can say that again," Dunkum said.

Shawn spoke up, too. "Jason is very good friend."

It came out like *velly* good.

But Jason didn't mind. Not one bit.

# BOOK 14

# Green Gravy

To
Claire Badger,
a delightful young reader
full of great story ideas.
(Thanks for "friendly freckles"!)

# One

**C**arly Hunter's stomach did a flip-flop.
She looked up from her school desk.

The teacher had just called her name. But Miss Hartman looked happy, not frowny.

"You're the student of the week!" she said to Carly.

"I am?" Carly couldn't believe her ears.

"Please come to the front of the room," Miss Hartman said.

Carly got up and walked toward the teacher's desk.

Dee Dee Winters, Carly's best friend, gave her a high five. "Three cheers for Carly Hunter!" she said.

The others joined in. "Three cheers," they chanted.

Carly smiled and turned to face her classmates.

The teacher pinned a button on her sweater. It said *Student of the Week*. The words *Blossom Hill School* were spelled out at the bottom.

Miss Hartman gave Carly a piece of paper. "Give this to your parents. They can help you gather information about your life," she said. "To share on your special day."

"Thank you," Carly replied.

*Wow!* This was going to be fun.

During the school year, Carly had paid close attention. Other students had been given this honor. To get picked, you had to be a good citizen. An extra good one.

Before she sat down, Miss Hartman explained some things. "As you know, the honored student makes a wish," she said. "It can be anything—within reason, of course."

For a moment, Carly thought. She glanced across the room at Dee Dee. Her friend was making hand motions.

What was she trying to say?

Dee Dee was pointing toward the wall calendar.

Carly looked at the calendar. She saw a big green clover. It marked St. Patrick's Day. March 17.

Now Dee Dee pointed to her own shirt. It was green-and-white checked.

The teacher was waiting. "Are you ready to make your wish?" she asked.

"I'm not sure," replied Carly.

She glanced at Dee Dee again.

Then she noticed Jimmy, her adopted Korean brother. He was leaning forward. His dark eyes were shining.

Carly could just imagine what he was thinking. *Wish for more recesses*, he might say.

But she stared at the calendar. She looked at the big green clover. She thought about St. Patrick's Day.

There was plenty of Irish on her mother's side of the family.

She looked around the room again.

Lots of kids here probably weren't Irish. Dee Dee was one of them. She had dark skin and deep brown eyes. Her hair had natural curls. Lucky for Dee Dee.

And there was Carly's adopted brother.

Jimmy had olive skin and straight, black hair. His eyes slanted up a little.

She took a breath and held it in.

Was her wish the right one?

Maybe not.

The teacher and the students were still waiting.

Carly decided to make a secret wish. It was a before-the-wish wish. The wish of a worrywart.

She wished that her *special* wish would be just right.

By now, Jimmy was wiggling in his seat.

Dee Dee wrinkled her nose.

Other students were restless, too.

At last, Carly breathed out all her air.

It was time.

The student of the week's wish was ready.

# TWO

Carly said, "My wish is . . ."

She looked at the calendar again. Today was Monday. Her special day was going to land on St. Patrick's Day!

On Wednesday. Just two more days.

"I want everyone to wear green," she said. "Because I'm Irish."

The kids started to clap.

All but Jimmy.

Their clapping made Carly smile.

That's when the greatest idea popped into her head.

"Oh, and one more thing," she said out loud.

The teacher looked surprised. "Only *one* wish."

Carly turned to her. "But this is lots like the other wish."

"Well, let's hear it." Miss Hartman leaned over so Carly could whisper in her ear.

"Everyone must eat green food for St. Patrick's Day," Carly whispered.

Miss Hartman stood up straight. She was smiling. "I don't see why we can't have this wish, too," she said. "It's a two-part wish. Part A and part B."

Then she told the class, "We'll all wear green clothes and eat green foods. Let's make Carly's wish come true."

Someone said, "Yucko." It was Jimmy. His hand shot up.

"Yes?" the teacher said.

"Everyone do this?" Jimmy asked. He was learning to speak English.

Miss Hartman nodded. "It's Carly's wish. And she's our student of the week."

Jimmy's cheeks sagged. "I not eat green food. I eat mashed potato and gravy." He held up the school menu. "I buy hot lunch on Carly Hunter day!" He shook his head and made a grumpy face.

Carly felt her neck getting hot. *Jimmy is a sourpuss brother*, she thought.

She wanted to stamp her foot and holler. But she walked to her desk and sat down.

She felt Dee Dee's hand on her shoulder. Dee Dee's desk was right behind hers.

"Jimmy's mad," whispered Dee Dee.

Carly looked over her shoulder. "That's his problem," she said.

Then she looked at Jimmy. He'd put his head down on his desk. She couldn't see his face.

"*Now* what?" Carly said, mostly to herself.

Jimmy was pouting again. He'd just have to get over it.

Since coming to the United States, Jimmy had learned lots of new things. Like about new holidays. He would have to go green for Carly's special day.

Whether he liked it or not!

■ ■ ■

It was after school.

Her mother waited at the front door. "How was your day?"

"I'm student of the week!" Carly exclaimed. "I have to tell the class all about my life."

She showed the paper with directions from Miss Hartman.

Mother smiled a happy face. "Would you like to show the class some baby pictures?"

"Yes!" Carly said. "And what else?"

"How about a picture of Snow White, our dog?" said Mother.

"Good idea!" Carly was excited. "And can I take Quacker to school?"

Her mother laughed. "A duck at school? I don't know about that."

"But she's my pet," Carly said. "She's part of the family."

Carly went to look outside. The ducks, Quacker and Jack, were in their pen. They waddled through the dirt. They pecked at their feed.

"Well . . . maybe you're right," she said. "Maybe it's not a good idea for a duck to go to school."

Her mother studied the teacher's idea list. "What about your favorite foods?" she said.

"Sweets," said Carly. "I love sweets."

"Then we'll bake cookies for everyone in your class," her mother said. She was checking off the list. "Can we fit everything

into a shoe box?" she asked. "Except the cookies, of course."

"We'll try," said Carly. "But not my duck."

Her mother agreed. "Definitely not."

"I know! I'll draw a picture of Quacker,"
Carly suggested. "We have art class tomorrow."

Her mother nodded. "I like that idea. Good
thinking."

Carly leaned over her mother's shoulder.
She looked at the list. "Anything else?"

"It would be nice to show pictures of your
family," her mother said.

Carly thought about that. "OK with me,"
she said. "But none of Jimmy."

Her mother gave her a strange look. "Why
not? He's your brother."

"But he's in my class," Carly said. "Everyone
knows what Jimmy looks like."

*He looks like a sourpuss,* she thought. *Because that's what he is!*

"Why don't you think about it," her mother
said.

"I'll think," Carly said. But she wasn't so
sure.

# Three

At supper, Jimmy poked at his food. Carly watched.

"Sit up and eat, son," their father said.

"No like peas," Jimmy said. He pushed his plate away.

Carly shook her head. "He's still upset."

Mother perked up her ears. "Why is that?"

"Because of me," Carly said.

Her big sister, Abby, frowned. "What did *you* do to him?"

Carly jerked her head and glared at Abby. "I didn't do anything. He's mad because I got picked for student of the week."

"Good going for Carly!" Shawn said. He was Jimmy's Korean brother. His big brother.

Now Shawn was glaring at Jimmy. "Not good being mad at little sister," Shawn said. He began to talk in Korean.

Jimmy covered his ears with his hands. "Carly make class wear green," he whined. "She make us eat yucko green food."

Abby and Shawn laughed.

So did their mother, but not very long.

Their father spoke up. "Wearing green might be fun."

"And just think of all the cool *green* foods there are," said Abby.

"Yeah, like celery," said Carly.

"And pears," Shawn said.

"Yucko," Jimmy said. His face was grumpy.

"Spinach has a nice green color," said their father. He was smiling now.

"So does broccoli," said Mother.

"Lettuce is green," said Carly.

"Yuck, yuck . . . yucko," chanted Jimmy.

Their father frowned. "I want you to practice eating green foods. Starting right now, with your peas."

Jimmy shot eye darts at Carly. He muttered something in Korean.

Then he picked up his spoon. One by one,

he shot the peas across the table. Right at Carly!

Mother's eyebrows popped up.

Father scooted his chair back. "Time out," he told Jimmy. "Let's have a talk in your bedroom."

Jimmy's face got all purple and red. He said, "Excuse, please," and left the table.

"Whew! He's in big trouble," Carly whispered.

Her mother put a finger to her lips. "Jimmy must learn to behave," she explained.

"He's a sourpuss," Carly said.

"Calling names won't help," Abby said.

Their mother agreed. "Let's be kind."

Carly nodded her head. Mother was always saying things like that. Good-citizen things.

"It's not easy to be nice all the time," Carly said.

"I understand," said Mother. "But it's good to keep trying."

Carly blinked her eyes. "You should have seen Jimmy pouting at school."

Mother patted Carly's long curls.

"I wish Daddy would come to school on St. Patrick's Day," Carly muttered.

"What for?" Abby asked.

"To make Jimmy wear green," said Carly. "And so he'll eat a green lunch."

"Who cares about that?" Abby said.

"I care," said Carly. "It's *my* special day!"

"You should hear yourself," said Abby. "If Jimmy's a sourpuss, what's that make you?"

"A sour *somebody*," answered Carly. She sat up straight and wiped her mouth with a napkin.

"Girls, girls," their mother said.

Abby got up from the table and went to the sink.

Carly wondered what her sister was thinking. She probably thought Miss Hartman should change her mind. Maybe someone else should be student of the week. Someone not so sour!

"Am I a sweet girl?" Carly asked her mother.

"Most of the time," Mother replied.

Abby returned to the table. "Nobody's perfect," she said.

"You think *you* are," Carly whispered.

Abby frowned. "That's not true!"

"Oh really?" Carly felt a fuss coming.

81

It seemed their mother did, too. "All right, you two. Clean up the kitchen." She went to the living room.

Carly carried two dishes to the sink. She spied the water sprayer and thought about spraying Abby.

When Abby wasn't looking, she picked up the sprayer.

She aimed.

"Better not," Shawn warned.

But Carly didn't listen.

*Swoosh!*

Water squirted the back of Abby's head.

"Hey!" Abby shouted.

Carly dropped the sprayer and ran to her bedroom.

She closed the door and pushed against it. "I'm a sour somebody," she whispered to herself.

She waited for Abby to pound on the door.

No sound came.

She counted to twenty-five.

Still nothing.

But soon, her mother's voice came through the door. "I need your help in the kitchen, please."

Slowly, Carly opened the door.

There stood her mother. And a drippy Abby.

"Somebody needs to say 'sorry,'" her mother said. "Then you may wipe up the kitchen floor."

Carly gulped.

She was *not* a good citizen. Not today.

# Four

It was Tuesday art class.

Carly loved art.

She liked to daydream before she made a picture.

Daydreaming was like night dreaming. Except it happened when you were awake. It was the best kind of dreaming, because you could plan it.

Sorta.

Carly stared out the art room window. Staring was a big part of daydreaming.

That's when she got an idea.

Another *green* idea!

Tomorrow was her special day. It was also St. Patrick's Day.

"I'll make a pinch rule," she whispered.

Dee Dee tapped her on the arm. "Who are you talking to?"

"Myself."

"How come?" asked Dee Dee.

"I'll tell you at recess."

"Tell me now," Dee Dee insisted.

"OK," Carly said. She whispered in Dee Dee's ear.

"What?" Dee Dee asked. "I didn't hear you."

The art teacher was coming. Time to get to work.

"Tell you later," said Carly.

She picked up her sketch pencil. She made a picture of Quacker, her pet duck.

Then Carly stopped drawing and looked at the sketch.

*Scrunch!* She wadded up the paper.

She tried again. This time, her duck looked like a too-fat bowling pin.

*Ducks are hard*, she decided.

So she daydreamed. And stared a lot.

She thought about tomorrow. She thought about the pinch rule.

Sourpuss Jimmy was sitting across the room.

She stared at him, too.

He didn't want to wear green tomorrow. He'd said so last night. He was going to spoil everything!

Now he was drawing something. He was working very hard.

When Jimmy looked up, she caught his eye.

Carly made a mad face. Capital M!

But Jimmy grinned back.

He held up his drawing. It was a clover leaf. A *red* one.

Whoever heard of that?

Carly knew he was making fun of her green-day idea.

*You'll be sorry*, she thought.

The pinch rule was going to be great.

By afternoon recess tomorrow, everyone would know about it.

Especially sourpuss Jimmy.

■■■

At recess, Carly and Dee Dee made a circle. A tiny, secret circle just big enough for two best friends.

Carly told her friend about the pinch rule. "Whoever isn't wearing green gets pinched," she said. "That's the pinch rule."

"Isn't the whole class gonna wear green?" Dee Dee asked.

"Jimmy's not," Carly replied.

"Then he's the only one who's gonna get pinched," said Dee Dee. But she wasn't laughing.

"I know." Carly grabbed a swing.

Dee Dee took the one next to her. "So why do you want to have a pinch rule?" she asked. "Is it 'cause of Jimmy?"

"Jimmy's a sourpuss. That's why!" Carly leaned back in her swing. She made it go high into the sky.

"I thought you liked Jimmy," Dee Dee shouted. "Ever since your parents adopted him, it's been you and him. Good friends."

Carly didn't say anything. She wished Dee Dee would keep quiet. Too many kids were standing around.

"Jimmy's your brother, remember?" Dee Dee said.

"I didn't say he wasn't," Carly hollered back.

Dee Dee dragged her feet and stopped swinging. She got off. And she stood right where Carly could see her.

But Carly stared up at the sky. "Quit bugging me," she said.

Dee Dee said, "Yes, Your Royal *High*ness."

Then she walked away.

"Oh, great," Carly whispered. "The student of the week has another enemy."

She—Carly Hunter—wasn't so special. She knew it for sure now.

So did her best friend.

And probably her brother.

She felt like crying.

# Five

It was Carly's special day.

"Make Jimmy wear green!" Carly wailed.

Her mother shook her head. "I'm not going to force him," she said. "Jimmy's Korean, not Irish."

"But he *has* to," Carly told her. "The whole class is supposed to wear green and eat green."

"Well, I gave Jimmy some lunch money," her mother said. "So it's up to the school cook, I guess."

Carly wanted to stamp her foot. But she knew better. Her mother would give her extra chores if she did.

She went to her room. She made her bed

and folded her pajamas. Cleaning up helped to take the M out of mad!

On top of that, she counted to fifty. Very slowly.

Soon, she was drawing another picture of Quacker. *This* time, she looked out the window at her duck. She took her time and did a good job.

The sketch turned out just ducky.

She pinned on her *Student of the Week* button.

Now she was ready to make her green lunch.

First, she washed two big pieces of celery. No peanut butter today. Wrong color.

Next, she put two pieces of lettuce together. She added sliced dill pickles.

She found some raw broccoli. A little avocado dip would taste good.

She helped herself to a handful of Spanish olives.

Her green meal was done. All but the drink.

A pouch of lemon-lime fruit drink was easy. Nice and green, too.

Before she left, she reached into the cookie jar.

*Yum!*

She'd helped her mother bake beautiful green clover cookies. With ooey-gooey green topping.

"There should be plenty for your classmates," her mother said.

"Teacher too?" Carly asked.

"Help yourself." Her mother found a plastic bag.

Carly put a bunch of cookies inside. "Maybe *now* Jimmy will eat something green," she said.

Her mother smiled. "Maybe, but maybe not."

"Why's he so stubborn?" asked Carly.

"Stubborn?" her mother said. "You could be wrong about that, dear. Jimmy might be feeling something else."

"Like what?" Carly asked. She couldn't think of anything.

"Jimmy needs to be himself," her mother said. "He's still getting used to living in this country. And to all of us." She kissed Carly good-bye. "Do you have your shoe box full of things?"

"In my room," Carly said. "I have everything I need for my special day."

*Everything but a best friend and a nice little brother*, she thought.

Without them, that added up to nothing much!

"Take good care of your pictures," her mother reminded her.

"I will," Carly said. "I promise."

"I'll carry the cookies," Abby said.

"Thank you," Carly said.

She was trying hard to be a good citizen.

■■■

Carly stuck with her big sister, Abby. And her big brother, Shawn. They walked across the street together.

Abby's best friend, Stacy Henry, and Eric Hagel came with them, too.

They were four of the older Cul-de-Sac Kids. The rest of the kids in the club were already at school.

Miss Hartman's outside door was super easy to see.

It was the one with all the green kids lined up. A ribbon of green stretched out across the playground.

Carly saw something else. Something purple.

*It's Jimmy*, she thought. *He's spoiling my day*.

"Make sure you don't drop your pictures," Abby said.

"Mommy already told me to be careful," Carly shot back.

"Hey, what's the matter?" Abby said. "I was only trying to help."

"Well, I don't need any help." Carly stamped off.

Abby couldn't stop her. It was OK to stamp in the school yard.

"Guess I'll just eat up your cookies!" Abby called.

Carly spun around. "No!"

Abby hurried over. "Here," she said. "I was only kidding."

"Don't be a sourpuss like Jimmy," Carly muttered to herself. Carefully, she carried the cookie bag and the shoe box.

Now . . . where was Dee Dee?

Carly searched. The line of green students was a problem. Everyone looked the same!

Finally, she found her friend. Dee Dee's natural curls had a big green bow.

Carly waved to her. But Dee Dee didn't wave back.

Neither did Jimmy. He was at the end of the line.

"You look nice and green," Carly said to her friend.

Dee Dee didn't smile. "So do you."

Something was strange about Dee Dee's voice. It sounded flat.

"What's the matter?" Carly asked.

"Nothin' much," Dee Dee said.

She always said that when she was upset.

Carly got in line behind her. But Dee Dee didn't turn around. She didn't even look at Carly's clover cookies!

*What's her problem?* she wondered.

Carly could hardly wait for the bell.

# Six

**M**iss Hartman was writing on the board. Her suit was bright green. Her blouse was all swirls of green and blue.

When everyone was seated, she called the roll.

Jimmy was the only one missing.

"Is your brother sick?" Miss Hartman asked Carly.

Carly turned around. She looked all around the room. "I just saw him at the end of the line," she said.

Dee Dee tapped her on the shoulder. "Look out the window. Jimmy's hiding."

Carly stretched up out of her seat.

Her brother was sitting on the slide.

"There he is!" Carly pointed.

"Oh dear," Miss Hartman said and rushed out the door.

Everyone jumped up to see.

Carly and Dee Dee got out of their seats, too.

"What's going on?" Dee Dee asked Carly.

"Who knows."

"Looks like Jimmy's got some markers," one girl called.

Everyone rushed to the window. They crowded in.

Carly was too short. She couldn't see.

Dee Dee crawled up on someone's desk. She started to giggle.

"What's funny?" Carly asked.

"Jimmy's painting dots on his nose," Dee Dee said.

"Dots? What for?" Carly asked.

"How would I know?" Dee Dee said.

The kids watched for a moment.

"Here comes the teacher!" someone said. "And Jimmy!"

They darted to their seats like scared mice.

Miss Hartman came inside, grinning. Silently, she guided Jimmy to his seat.

Carly stared. She knew she wasn't daydreaming.

Now everyone was staring.

Dee Dee was right. Jimmy *did* have dots on his nose.

But they weren't just any kind of dots.

They were GREEN ones!

"Those are some strange freckles," one boy joked.

Jimmy spoke up. "Friendly freckles." He laughed.

Miss Hartman sat at her desk. "Quiet, class," she said.

Everyone settled down.

"Every student in this class has helped make Carly's wish come true," Miss Hartman said. "Happy St. Patrick's Day."

The kids chattered a bit. They were saying "Happy St. Patrick's Day" to each other.

But Carly wasn't. She was staring at Jimmy.

His friendly green freckles went all across his nose. They spilled over onto his cheeks.

Carly was no dummy. She could see right through those sourpuss freckles.

Jimmy had tricked her. On purpose!

He'd tricked her with those green freckles.

She couldn't use the pinch rule on him.

It was no good now.

*Rats!*

# Seven

It was time for morning recess.

Miss Hartman's class flew out the side door.

"Jimmy's a smart one," Dee Dee said. "He's wearing green, after all."

"Whose side are you on?" asked Carly.

Dee Dee didn't say anything. She rubbed her ear.

Carly stared at her.

"Not nice to stare," Dee Dee said.

"I want to know whose side you're on," Carly said.

Dee Dee sniffed. But she didn't talk.

"Aw, c'mon," Carly pleaded. "Talk to me."

Dee Dee shook her head. "Only if you fix things up."

"With who?" Carly asked.

"You know who," Dee Dee said. "Start treating your brother nicer!"

Carly felt a fuss coming. "You can't tell me what to do, Dee Dee Winters!"

She dashed to the swings.

Dee Dee ran the opposite way. She went in Miss Hartman's classroom door.

"You're a squealer," Carly said out loud. She stamped her foot.

"Who's tattling?"

Carly turned her head.

There stood Abby and Stacy.

"Are you fighting with Dee Dee?" Abby asked.

Carly pouted. "Nobody's business."

Abby sat on the swing next to her. "You look pretty today," she said. "I like your green polka-dot skirt."

Carly shook her head. "I know what you're doing," she said. "I'm no dummy."

"Didn't say you were," Abby told her.

"So why are you saying I look pretty?" Carly asked.

"Listen to me," her big sister said. "You're the student of the week, right?"

Carly nodded. She bit her lower lip. "Guess you don't think I oughta be."

Stacy stepped up. She leaned close to Carly's face. "Abby didn't mean that. You're a good citizen, Carly."

"Just not a *perfect* citizen," said Carly.

Abby scratched her head. "Don't say that."

Stacy glanced at Abby and lifted her shoulders. "Here comes someone," she said.

Carly looked up. Dee Dee was coming toward them.

"Hey, look, she's smiling," Abby said.

"It's a sourpuss smile," said Carly. "I know a squealer when I see one!"

# Eight

The bell rang. Morning recess was over.
Carly hurried inside the classroom.
She looked at Miss Hartman's face.

*Is she upset?* Carly wondered.

She couldn't tell for sure.

Carly turned around in her seat. "Why did
you squeal?" she asked Dee Dee.

"I just said what *you* said," Dee Dee replied. "And Miss Hartman said that it wasn't
very nice."

Carly muttered, "Especially for a good citizen."

"What?" Dee Dee said.

"Nothing," replied Carly. She wanted to cry.

Nothing was turning out right. Nothing
at all.

Jimmy was getting away with wearing
purple.

Dee Dee was mad with a capital M!

Miss Hartman was taking sides.

And . . . oh no!

She was putting good-citizen stars beside Jimmy's name. Up on the board where everyone could see.

*Why?* she wondered. *Jimmy doesn't deserve stars!*

She felt Dee Dee tapping her back. "Look. Jimmy's earning points," Dee Dee said.

Carly didn't turn around.

How could Miss Hartman do this?

Dee Dee kept whispering. "Jimmy didn't want to wear green, remember? He's not Irish one bit! But he followed your wish, Carly. He put green freckles on his nose. Now, *that's* a good citizen."

"Sh-h!" said Miss Hartman. "It's time for our student of the week. Carly Hunter, will you please come forward?"

Carly was upset. She twisted the eraser off her pencil.

*Ka-pop!*

It sailed over Dee Dee's desk and landed on Jimmy's head.

"What was that?" asked the teacher.

Jimmy felt the top of his head. He found the round pink ball. "Eraser drop down from sky," he said.

The kids laughed.

Carly froze. Now what?

Miss Hartman went around the room. She looked at everyone's pencil.

She came to Carly's desk and looked at her pencil.

The pink top was missing.

Carly looked down. "I didn't mean to," she said. "It was a mistake."

Dee Dee giggled behind her. "That's what erasers are for—mistakes!"

Everyone was laughing even harder.

Suddenly, Carly felt sick. "Excuse me," she said.

Off she ran to the girls' room.

■■■

Carly turned on the water. Cold water.

She slapped some on her face.

Then she dried off with a paper towel.

The face in the bathroom mirror was a grumpy face. Capital G!

"What's the matter with me?" she asked out loud.

Soon, Miss Hartman came in. "Are you all right?"

Carly shook her head. "I don't know."

"Maybe the nurse should check you," said her teacher.

Miss Hartman took her to the little square room. It smelled like mushroom soup.

The nurse had her sit down. She checked for a fever. She made her say "Ahh!"

"You seem normal," the nurse said. "Maybe a little rest will help."

"OK. I'll rest," Carly said. She went to the cot to lie down.

But rest was impossible. Things were on her mind. Things like green foods and lunchtime. And Jimmy's not-green hot lunch.

She thought about the pinch rule. It was kerplooey.

Why not a lunch rule, too? A rule for anyone who didn't eat green foods.

Like sourpuss Jimmy!

She looked at the clock. It wouldn't be long now until lunch.

Would her brother trick her again?

# Nine

Carly stared at the wall in the nurse's room.

She let herself daydream.

Jimmy had a sour-apple pie smashed on his head. It had rotten green apples in it. And long green worms.

Carly shivered. She took a breath.

"How are you feeling?" asked the nurse.

"I need a drink of water, please," Carly said.

The nurse helped her up.

"Thank you," said Carly.

The lady let the water run. She gave her the full glass.

"Is it time for lunch yet?" Carly asked.

"Almost," said the nurse. "Are you hungry?"

Carly nodded and scooted off the cot. "I think I'm better now."

The nurse walked her back to Miss Hartman's room. "Tell your teacher if you're sick again."

"Thank you very much," Carly answered.

The nurse smiled. "What a polite girl."

"Thank you." Carly smiled, too.

The nurse was right. She *was* polite. Most of the time.

Carly opened the classroom door.

Miss Hartman was checking papers.

Quickly, Carly went to her seat and took out her notebook.

"We're making P's and D's today in handwriting," Miss Hartman told her. "For St. Patrick's Day."

Carly made her letters curly.

"That's not right," Dee Dee said in her ear.

But Carly didn't turn around. She made seven more letters. Each one curlier than the last.

When Jimmy wasn't looking, Carly stared at him. She could see his paper. He was drawing a clover leaf at the top.

A green one!

Would he eat a green lunch, too?

■■■

At last, it was lunchtime.

Miss Hartman's green students walked to the cafeteria.

Carly watched Jimmy. She didn't let him out of sight.

"Feeling better?" asked Dee Dee. She didn't wait for Carly to answer. "Still mad at your brother?"

"Not nice to be nosy," Carly answered.

She headed to a different table. Abby and Stacy were sitting there. Jason Birchall and Dunkum Mifflin were there, too. And Shawn, of course.

"Hi, Carly," they all said.

"Can I sit here?" she asked.

"Well, I don't know if you *can*, but you may," Stacy said.

Carly smiled. Stacy liked to correct the way kids talked. She had the best grammar in the cul-de-sac.

"Why aren't you sitting with your class?" Abby asked.

Carly lifted one shoulder. "Don't wanna."

She kept looking over at Jimmy. He was in the hot-lunch line now. And it looked like his friendly freckles were gone.

Carly thought about the lunch rule. "Is there any green food for hot lunch?" she asked.

Stacy laughed. "Our cook's not *that* creative."

"Well, I am!" Jason Birchall said. He held up a long, skinny tube. "This is my dessert."

Jason didn't just like the color green; he loved it. Especially green things like bullfrogs. Dill pickles, too.

Carly looked at the long tube. "What's that?" she asked.

"It's cake icing," Jason said. "Wanna squeeze?"

"Maybe later," Carly said.

She stared at Jason's lunch. It was definitely a St. Patrick's Day meal. There were bunches of green grapes, slices of green melon, and a cup of green Jell-O. And a giant dill pickle.

"Hey, you're eating all green foods," she said.

"Green as a bean!" Jason poked his pointer fingers in the air and jerked his head around.

The kids at the table laughed. So did Carly.

"Green as a bean!" they joined in.

Kids were looking at them. Mostly Miss Hartman's class, on the other side of the cafeteria.

Carly didn't mind.

She opened her lunch bag. She stopped long enough to glance across at her younger brother.

Jimmy had just set down his lunch tray.

Carly could see his plate. There was brown meat and gravy and some white mashed potatoes. The other vegetable was orange. Carrots!

Nice colors, but the wrong ones!

Stacy was right. The school cook wasn't very creative. Or maybe she wasn't Irish.

"There isn't a scrap of hot green food anywhere!" Carly said.

Stacy and Abby nodded. "That's true," said Stacy.

"Isn't anybody else celebrating St. Patrick's Day?" Carly asked.

Abby teased, "Looks like part B of your wish isn't working."

"Hey!" Carly turned to her sister. "Do you have to tell the whole world?"

Abby just smiled. "It's kinda cute, that's all."

"Not *cute*," Carly said. "Cute's for babies." And she slid off her seat.

"Hey, don't forget your green lunch," Abby called.

"Forget you!" Carly snapped.

She picked up her lunch bag. Then she marched to the other side of the cafeteria.

# Ten

Carly went to Jimmy's table and sat down. She glanced around at the lunches.

Everyone in her class was having green stuff for lunch. There was split pea soup and lots of celery sticks. One girl even had some fresh spinach!

No one at their table was having hot lunch. No one except Jimmy.

He didn't seem to care about her wish. Part A or part B. Nope. He sprinkled some salt and pepper on his gravy and dug right in.

"How's it taste?" Carly asked him.

"Very good." It sounded like *velly* good.

Carly stared at his tray. "Nothing's green on your plate," she whined.

Jimmy nodded. "I not eat green. I *not* Irish."

"Where are your friendly freckles?" she asked.

"Not like green dot face," he said.

The boy next to Jimmy laughed.

Jimmy joined in.

That did it!

Carly leaped up. She flew across the cafeteria to Abby's table.

Jason's tube of cake icing was in plain view.

"Mind if I squeeze this?" she asked.

Jason didn't have a chance to answer. She was gone before he could say *"St. Patrick's Day."*

At Jimmy's table, Carly hid the icing behind her. She hurried around to Jimmy. "I get my wish!" she said.

She leaned over Jimmy's shoulder.

And . . .

*Squeeze!*

Out came the gooey green icing.

*Plop!*

It landed in Jimmy's gravy.

"Eew!" The kids at the table groaned.

"Happy St. Patrick's Day!" she singsonged to her brother.

Jimmy's eyes were big now. Not angry, just big.

Slowly, he picked up his fork and took a bite.

The kids watched. They leaned toward him.

Dee Dee moved over to their table. She wanted to see what was going on.

"How's it taste *now*?" teased Carly.

"Green gravy not bad," Jimmy said.

He took another bite.

Dee Dee said, "I can't believe he's eating it."

"Green gravy good stuff," Jimmy said. "I not Irish, but I eat green gravy!"

Miss Hartman's kids chanted, "Green gravy . . . green gravy . . ."

Across the cafeteria, Abby and her friends were staring.

Carly didn't mind.

She went around and squeezed green icing on pickles, Jell-O, and spinach. She squeezed it on lettuce and green pears.

It was a double dabble lunchtime. That's exactly what Abby would say.

Jason Birchall came running over. "Hey, don't use it all," he hollered.

"Thanks for the big squeeze," Carly said. She gave him the smashed-up tube. "You made my green wish come true."

Jason jigged around and acted silly. Then he trailed a string of icing onto his tongue.

Now all the kids were looking at *Jason*.

The lunchroom teacher blew a whistle.

*Yikes.* Carly hurried to sit down.

"Quiet!" the teacher called.

Everyone tried to settle down. It wasn't easy.

The kids at Jimmy's table were holding in the giggles.

The kids at Abby's table were tasting Jason's icing.

Carly was having too much fun.

She forgot all about the lunch rule.

# Eleven

**C**arly carried her shoe box to Miss Hart-man's desk.

She set down her bag of green cookies.

The teacher said, "There are fifteen stars beside Carly's name. She has earned the good citizenship award."

Carly took a deep breath. She hoped she hadn't let her teacher down. Or her class-mates.

"Everyone listen carefully," said Miss Hart-man. She nodded for Carly to begin.

"My name is Carly Anne Hunter," Carly said. "My middle name is *always* spelled with an 'e' on the end. I was born seven years ago. And I'm Irish on my mother's side."

She showed a picture of a fluffy white

puppy. "This is Snow White. She's the color of clean snow."

Next, Carly held up a drawing of her duck. "This is Quacker," she said. "Her brother's name is Jack. Quacker and Jack are brother and sister."

The girls giggled.

The boys tried not to.

Someone asked, "Do your ducks fight?"

Carly nodded her head. "Like cats and dogs," she said.

She was ready to talk about her favorite foods. "I like sweets best." The clover cookies got passed around.

She noticed that Jimmy took two.

At last, she showed her family picture. "This is the whole Hunter family," she said.

She pointed to each person, starting with her parents. "My father's English and my mother's Irish. But they learned to like Korean food these past months."

Next, she pointed to Abby. "This is my big sister. She's the president of the Cul-de-Sac Kids. It's a club. Abby makes up words like 'double dabble.'"

Carly pointed to a tall, skinny boy. "Shawn's

nine years old. He plays soccer and the violin. His Korean name is Li Sung Jin, and he's my adopted big brother. Snow White is really *his* pet."

She picked up the dog's picture again.

Miss Hartman asked a question. "Is Snow White a Shih Tzu?"

"Yes," Carly answered. "Her doggie family tree goes back to ancient China."

"Do you know what Shih Tzu means?" asked the teacher.

"My father told me," Carly said. "It means *Lion Dog*. These pets were watchdogs in the Chinese royal courts."

"Wow," someone whispered.

"Cool," someone else said.

Carly spoke up. "But better than all that is someone in this class. Someone very special." She pointed to Jimmy and asked him to stand up.

"You all know Jimmy. He's my adopted brother. He's Shawn's birth brother."

Jimmy was smiling.

"Will you come stand with me?" she asked him.

Her brother nodded. "I come."

Carly smiled at Jimmy. "Here is the best citizen I know," she said. "And a good sport."

She told about the green gravy. For Miss Hartman's sake.

Then she turned to Jimmy. "I'm sorry for being selfish and a sourpuss. A good citizen is *not* selfish."

She took off her *Student of the Week* pin.

She put it on Jimmy.

Miss Hartman was smiling the biggest smile.

Everyone else was clapping.

Except Jimmy.

He pulled out his marker.

"What are you going to do?" Carly asked.

"I draw Irish green heart on sister face," he said. "Happy Carly Day!"

Carly felt like crying.

Happy tears. With a capital H!

And she never ever called Jimmy a sourpuss again.

# BOOK 15

# Backyard Bandit Mystery

For
Rochelle Glöege,
my editor and friend.
Happy birthday!

I know a fine editor—Rochelle,
Her excellent work I must tell.
She edits; she writes,
Stays up late some nights.
What a wonderful person, Rochelle.

B. L.

# One

**S**tacy Henry couldn't sleep.

*Whew!* Too hot.

She was supposed to be sleeping in the teeny-weeny attic. With a teeny-tiny window that didn't open.

Stacy didn't mind, because her grandparents were visiting. They were staying in her bedroom.

But such heat! The attic bedroom was way too hot.

She fanned herself with a pillow.

She tried counting sheep. But thinking of sheep's wool made her hotter.

Some fresh air would be nice. Some cool air.

Stacy sat up and lifted her hair off her neck.

Her puppy opened his eyes.

"I need a ponytail," she told him. "My head's too sweaty."

Sunday Funnies seemed to understand. He stood up and shook himself.

Stacy got out of bed and went to the hallway.

Fuzzy little Sunday Funnies followed.

They stood at the top of the steps and listened.

The house was quiet.

"Everyone's asleep," she whispered to the pup.

Then . . .

*Tippity pat-pat.* She crept downstairs.

*Jingle pat-pat.* Sunday Funnies came along.

Suddenly, Stacy stopped. So did her pup.

They heard a low rumble.

Grandpa was snoring. He said he got his best sleep that way.

"Let's be quiet," Stacy said to Sunday Funnies.

She tiptoed down the hall.

*Flap-flop.* Stacy's slippers slapped against her feet. They were big enough for an elephant. She tossed them off and went barefoot.

Inside her own room, Stacy sneaked past the round, snoring bodies. She hurried to the dresser.

Silently, she pulled open the top drawer. There, she found her hairbrush and a rubber band.

Then she went outside.

The top step was cooler than the wooden porch.

Stacy sat there and looked at the streetlight.

She wished for a breeze.

But the night was still. Breathless.

She brushed her hair back and made a ponytail.

*Ah!* Much better.

Sunday Funnies sat at her bare feet.

Stacy glanced down at him. "Some night we should sleep outside," she said. "It would be lots cooler."

She leaned back and stared at the sky.

"The Cul-de-Sac Kids oughta have a sleep-out this summer," she said.

Sunday Funnies went and rolled in the cool grass.

"Smart boy," Stacy said.

She looked up and down Blossom Hill Lane.

The houses were dark. Middle-of-the-night dark.

No lights shone from the windows. No sounds sprang from the doorways.

The whole cul-de-sac seemed gloomy.

Her best friend, Abby Hunter, was away camping this weekend. Abby's house next door looked lonely.

Stacy missed her friend.

She wondered if Abby was asleep yet. Or was *she* too hot? Or maybe homesick?

Stacy stared at the other houses.

Jason Birchall's was across the street.

Mr. Tressler's house was next door to Stacy's, at the far end of the cul-de-sac.

Eric Hagel's house was between Mr. Tressler's and Jason's houses.

Dee Dee Winters' and Dunkum Mifflin's houses were at the other end of the cul-de-sac.

Besides being dark, the houses looked dull. Boring!

Stacy was thinking about Flag Day. Next Friday.

The houses on Blossom Hill Lane needed some American flags.

But Stacy was broke. She couldn't afford even *one* flag.

"Ps-st," she whispered to Sunday Funnies. "I know what we need. A yard sale! For all the Cul-de-Sac Kids. Then we'll have enough money to buy flags!"

Her puppy jumped up and ran to her. He licked her face.

"Good idea, huh?" she said.

Then she glanced at Abby's house next door.

"Rats, it won't work," she said. "Abby's gone. The president of the Cul-de-Sac Kids has to call the meeting. And we *all* have to vote."

Sunday Funnies squirmed in her arms.

"It was such a great idea," Stacy said sadly. "Too bad."

# TWO

It was early Saturday morning.

The sun peeked through the teeny-weeny attic window.

*Yikes!* Stacy felt warm licks on her face. Sunday Funnies was wide-awake.

"OK," she laughed. "I get the message."

As soon as Stacy yawned, she remembered her idea.

"I'm gonna talk to Dunkum today," she said.

Dunkum's real name was Edward Mifflin. He was the tallest and best hoop shooter around. Everyone called him Dunkum.

"Maybe we could have a club meeting after all," she told her cockapoo.

But Stacy felt funny inside. Abby and her brothers and sister were part of the club, too. It wouldn't be fair to vote without them.

Would it?

Sunday Funnies turned his head and looked up at her. He seemed to think her idea was OK.

Stacy wasn't too sure. She'd have to check with Dunkum. *He* would know what to do.

■■■

Stacy couldn't wait to finish breakfast.

She poured a glass of juice. Then she sliced a banana on her cereal.

At last, she hurried down to Dunkum's house.

He was outside shooting baskets. "Hi, Stacy. What's up?" he asked.

"I have a great idea," she said.

He stopped shooting. "What is it?"

"We need to have a club meeting," she told him.

"Right now?" He glanced up the street. "Looks like the rest of the Cul-de-Sac Kids are sleeping in."

"Summers and Saturdays," she said under her breath.

"What's the meeting about?" he asked.

Stacy told him the Flag Day idea. "We need to jazz up Blossom Hill Lane," she said. "With flags."

Dunkum grinned. "Cool!"

"Only one problem. We have no money," she said.

"There's a little in the club fund," Dunkum said. He put his ball down and ran into the house.

Stacy hoped there was enough money to buy seven flags.

She looked at the houses again.

Flags would really spiff things up.

She crossed her fingers.

■■■

Stacy waited.

And waited.

And waited some more.

*What's taking so long?* she wondered.

At last, Dunkum came outside.

His face looked like a prune.

"What's wrong?" Stacy asked.

"I counted the money twice." Dunkum shrugged his shoulders. "I thought there was more."

"How much *is* there?" asked Stacy.

"Only two dollars and fifty-three cents. Mostly dimes and nickels," replied Dunkum.

Stacy uncrossed her fingers. "Not enough for seven flags."

"Not even close." Dunkum picked up his basketball.

"What about a fund raiser?" said Stacy. "A yard sale . . . at my house? This afternoon?"

Dunkum was silent. He aimed high, shot, and made it.

He looked at her. "Abby's gone," he said. "We can't vote without our president."

"I thought of that, too," said Stacy. "Besides, Carly, Shawn, and Jimmy aren't here to vote, either."

"You're right," Dunkum said.

She watched him make some fancy moves.

"Well, what if we broke the rules? Just once?" she suggested.

Dunkum kept shooting. Finally, he said, "Abby probably wouldn't mind."

"Should we talk to the others about it?" she asked.

Dunkum nodded. "Wanna?"

"Why not, right?" Stacy said with a grin.

But she had a strange feeling.

They'd never done *this* before!

# Three

Stacy stared at the president's beanbag chair. Abby Hunter's seat.

*Poof!* Stacy sat down too hard.

"The meeting will come to order," she said.

Dee Dee raised her hand. "Is this a real meeting?" She looked around the room. "Because if it is, four of us are missing."

Stacy nodded. "You're right."

Dunkum tried to explain things to little Dee Dee. "We want to buy some flags for Flag Day." He glanced over at Stacy. "It's a great idea. We just want to talk about it."

Eric Hagel and Jason Birchall both said they liked the idea.

"Why do we have to vote?" Jason asked.

"Yeah," said Eric. "Abby doesn't care if we make some money. It would be a good surprise!"

"When the cat's away, the mice will *pay*," Jason said.

Dee Dee giggled at the pun.

Stacy didn't laugh. "So, is it settled?" she asked everyone.

Five heads nodded *yes*.

"Well, are we gonna vote?" Dunkum asked.

"Go for it!" shouted Jason.

"OK," said Stacy. "How many are in favor of a yard sale?"

Five hands went up.

"How many want the yard sale to start today?" she asked.

Same five hands.

"Yes!" said Dunkum. "We're in business."

"Yay!" Stacy said. "Let's start gathering up our old loot. Anything we don't want."

"Hey! Your trash could be *my* treasure," Jason teased.

Dunkum and Eric agreed.

So did the girls.

"This'll be so-o cool," Dee Dee said.

"I'm gonna search for hidden treasure,"
Eric said. And he went right home.

So did everyone else.

■■■

Stacy hurried into the house. "Do we have
anything to sell?" she asked her mom.

"Like what?" her mom asked, smiling.

"You know, junk or old treasures. For a
yard sale," Stacy said.

Her mother thought for a moment. "I don't
think so," she said.

"Please look," Stacy pleaded.

"What's the sale for?" asked her mother.

"Money for Flag Day," answered Stacy.
"The Cul-de-Sac Kids want to buy flags for
every house on the block."

"Flags?" said Grandpa. "What a nice idea."

Stacy smiled. "I thought so, too."

"Where will you put the flags?" asked her
granny.

"On all the porches," Stacy explained.

Grandpa got off the couch and headed
down the hall.

"Where are you going, dear?" asked Granny.

"To scout around," Grandpa said.

"Where?" Granny asked.

"In my suitcase," Grandpa answered.

Granny's eyebrows flew up. "Oh no!"

"It's OK," Stacy said. "I'm sure he'll find something."

"That's what I'm afraid of," replied Granny.

"I'll go help him," Stacy offered.

Now her mother was frowning. "Better let Grandpa do his own looking," she said.

Stacy glanced at Granny. She was *really* frowning now.

"Sorry," Stacy said quietly.

She knew she had better stay out of it.

So she went to the attic.

It was time for some scouting of her own.

# Four

Later, Stacy and Grandpa hid out in the attic.

Some of their old treasures were piled on the bed.

"Don't let Granny catch you with these," Grandpa whispered.

Stacy looked through her grandpa's things.

There was a bottle of men's cologne, nearly full.

Stacy twisted off the cap and gave it a sniff. "Don't you want this?" she asked.

"Never liked the smell," he said with a grin. "Granny's the one who bought it."

Stacy shrugged. "Won't she be upset?"

"Ah, she'll get over it." He waved his hand.

"What if she doesn't?" Stacy asked.

"She'll just have to buy it back." He was laughing.

Next, he held up his pajama top.

"I think you might need that, Grandpa," said Stacy.

He laughed. "In this heat? No chance!"

It *was* hot for June. Especially June in Colorado.

"Just skip the pajama top and sleep in your undershirt," Stacy suggested.

"Hallelujah!" said Grandpa.

And he went downstairs.

*I don't want to get in trouble*, thought Stacy.

But she wasn't too worried. She remembered what Grandpa said. If Granny missed his stuff, she could just buy it back.

*Hallelujah!*

■■■

Before lunch, Dee Dee came over.

Stacy showed off some of her treasures. She showed some of her not-so-great treasures, too.

There was an old fishbowl.

Used magazines.

Some baby books with thick pages.

A cloth angel doll with wings.

Three sets of skirts and blouses. Two sweaters.

Dee Dee held up one of the skirts. "I like this one," she said.

"It's not for sale . . . not yet," Stacy said.

Dee Dee folded the skirt and put it away. "What about this?" She held up the angel. "It's real cute."

Stacy nodded. "Abby gave me that a long time ago."

"Don't you want it anymore?" asked Dee Dee. "It's so-o sweet."

"I'm tired of it," Stacy said.

Dee Dee played with the angel. She made it fly around. "What'll Abby say?" she asked.

Stacy laughed. "Abby won't care about an angel doll."

"Are you sure?" Dee Dee asked.

"Of course," Stacy replied. "Besides, it's really old."

Dee Dee put the angel back in the pile. "OK, then."

"Let's see *your* things," said Stacy.

Dee Dee's face lit up. She pulled out an old cat collar.

"This was Mister Whiskers' baby collar," she said. "Think it'll sell?"

"Sure will," Stacy replied.

There was more. Several old books of guitar music.

Three stuffed animals—a parrot, a fish, and a bee.

And a pink piggy bank.

"You've got some good stuff," Stacy told Dee Dee.

Dee Dee smiled. "Wait till you see Dunkum's loot."

"Really?" Stacy said.

"Come with me," said Dee Dee.

And the two of them hurried down the cul-de-sac.

■■■

Dunkum had a bunch, all right.

There were two baseball gloves.

Toy cars and trucks—a box full.

A stack of comic books.

And an old radio with star-shaped antennas.

"Nice things," Stacy said.

"Not to me," Dunkum said. "I've got new toys."

Dee Dee picked up the old radio. "Does this work?"

Dunkum plugged it in, and music blared out.

Dee Dee clicked her fingers to the beat. "Cool," she said.

Then Stacy, Dee Dee, and Dunkum headed to Eric's house.

"I wonder if Eric's grandpa gave him anything for the sale," Stacy said.

"How come?" Dunkum asked as they walked.

"Well, I was thinking about my grandpa's pajama top," she said. "It would be nice if someone donated a bottom."

"A *what?*" Dee Dee giggled.

Dunkum laughed, too.

Stacy tried to explain. But they were laughing too hard.

At last, they stopped.

Stacy told about her grandpa and his pajamas. "He gets too warm in the summertime," she said.

"He oughta sleep in his *birthday suit!*" Dee Dee said.

Stacy and Dunkum howled. They laughed so hard, they could barely walk.

They passed Jason Birchall's house. Next door was Eric's house.

Jason and his frog were at Eric's, too. "What's so funny?" Jason asked. "I heard you laughing all the way up the cul-de-sac."

Dee Dee told about the pajama problem. "We need a complete set of pj's for the yard sale."

Jason looked confused. "What's so funny about that?"

Dunkum tried not to laugh. "Maybe we'll borrow *your* pj's, Jason."

Jason rolled his eyes and backed away. "Whoa, don't look at me!" he said. "I like to cook breakfast in my pajamas."

"Isn't that kinda messy?" Eric teased him. "Why don't you use a frying pan?"

Now they were all laughing, even Jason.

Stacy glanced up the street. "Hey, look," she said.

The kids turned to see where she was pointing.

"Mr. Tressler's got pajamas," she said. "I can see them from here."

The striped pj's were hanging on the clothesline.

"I wonder if Mr. Tressler wants to donate something," Dunkum said.

"Let's go find out," Jason said.

Stacy and Dunkum looked at each other.

"Why don't *you* ask him?" they said to Jason.

Jason shook his head. "This wasn't my idea."

"OK, I'll go," Dee Dee said.

She started down the sidewalk. Then she turned back.

"What am I supposed to say?" she asked.

Stacy sighed. "C'mon. I'll go with you."

And she did.

# Five

It was the middle of the afternoon. Time for the yard sale.

The sun was hot.

Stacy made lemonade for everyone.

Dunkum brought a folding table.

Eric borrowed his mother's old tablecloth.

Jason brought a long extension cord to plug in Dunkum's radio.

"Music always livens things up," Jason said.

Everyone agreed.

Dee Dee sat in the grass and made a sale sign. She drew the letters carefully.

Dunkum watched. "The *e*'s are backward," he told her.

Stacy went over to look. "Who cares?" she said. "We're just kids, right?"

Dee Dee smiled up at Stacy. "You're nice," Dee Dee said.

Stacy picked up the sign. "You did an excellent job."

Dee Dee got up and stuck the sign on the tablecloth.

"We need some nickels, dimes, and pennies," Dunkum said.

"What for?" Jason asked.

"To make money, we have to start with some," Dunkum explained. "We might need to make change."

"What about the two dollars and fifty-three cents in our club fund?" asked Stacy.

"Good thinking," Dunkum said. He dashed out the backyard gate.

Together, Dee Dee and Stacy arranged the sale table.

They displayed Mr. Tressler's striped pj top. Stacy put it beside her grandpa's green pajama top.

"Now we've got two tops and no bottoms," Dee Dee said.

Stacy and Dee Dee giggled about it. They had fun sorting everything.

Stacy stepped back for a look. "This is really a good idea," she said.

Dee Dee grinned. "If you must say so yourself!"

"Well, it's *my* idea," said Stacy.

"That's just what I mean," Dee Dee said.

Jason came over and turned up the radio. He danced around. Then he said, "Let someone else toot your horn, Stacy."

"Oh, I get it," Stacy muttered. She felt silly about bragging.

Real silly.

■■■

The Cul-de-Sac Kids posted signs all over Blossom Hill Lane.

They told their parents. And their friends.

Now they were ready for customers. Lots of them.

Stacy could almost see the flags flying. Seven beautiful flags for Flag Day.

The Cul-de-Sac Kids waited.

And waited.

The sun got hotter.

And hotter.

They poured glasses of lemonade. One after another.

"We oughta charge ourselves for the drinks," Dee Dee said.

Dunkum nodded. "Why didn't I think of that?"

Stacy agreed. "It would be *one* way to make money."

"Yeah, because nobody's showing up," Dee Dee said.

Eric wiped his forehead. "It's too hot; that's why."

"We need some shade," Dunkum suggested.

Stacy remembered something in the attic. "I might have just what we need." She darted into the house.

Upstairs, she crawled on her knees. She looked under the little attic bed.

There it was.

She stretched her arm as far as she could.

The old striped canvas wasn't very big, but it might work.

Now she needed some tools.

She called for Grandpa. "I need a little help."

Grandpa came to the attic in his undershirt

and some red shorts. He was very round in certain places.

Stacy tried not to stare.

It was too hot for Grandpa to care.

"Here we are." He found just what they needed: a hammer and nails.

Grandpa headed for the kitchen door.

Stacy stopped. "Uh, are you going outside?" she asked.

Grandpa curled the canopy under one arm. "Show me where you want this thing," he said.

Stacy took a deep breath. Grandpa was going out dressed like *that*!

She held the door open for him. And she carried the hammer and nails outside.

Grandpa called, "Hey, kids!"

Everyone turned to look.

"You're going to have yourselves some shade," he told them.

The Cul-de-Sac Kids cheered.

"Hooray for Stacy's grandpa," Jason said.

Stacy put on a smile. She tried not to think about Grandpa's too-small undershirt.

"I'll help," Dee Dee said. She and Stacy found a ladder in the garage.

Dunkum and Eric carried it to the sale table.

Grandpa stepped on the bottom rung. He shook it around. The shaking made his stomach jiggle. Some of the other chunky places did, too.

Eric steadied the ladder.

Grandpa laughed. "How old's this thing, anyway?"

"Be careful," Stacy warned him. Then she handed the hammer up to him.

The boys helped Grandpa with the canvas. They stretched it over some boards and hammered away.

Jason and Dee Dee passed up the nails, one by one.

Stacy held her breath till the job was done.

"Awesome idea!" Jason said, looking at it.

"It's like an awning," Stacy said. "Thanks, Grandpa."

"Any old time," he said.

Then he went inside the house.

The kids hollered their thank-yous.

Now they could have their super sale.

In the shade.

*Grandpa's real cool*, thought Stacy.

# Six

It was late in the afternoon.

"We're running out of lemonade," Jason said.

"I'll make some more," said Stacy. She hurried to the house.

Grandpa was sitting near the kitchen fan. "Any customers yet?" he asked.

"It's too hot, but they'll come," Stacy said.

Granny came in the room. "Who's coming to what?" she asked.

Stacy explained about the yard sale. "Go out and have a look," she said.

"Don't mind if I do," Granny said.

But Grandpa was waving his hands at Stacy. He was trying to signal her.

Stacy finally caught on. "Oh . . . uh," she started to say.

Too late. Granny was already heading for her purse.

"Sorry about that," Stacy told Grandpa. "I forgot."

He shook his head. "Who knows? Maybe she won't spot my old things."

Stacy laughed. "Granny's real sharp. She'll notice, all right."

Soon, Granny came back with her cane and her purse. "I'm gonna have me some fun," she said.

Out she went.

Grandpa went to the window. He stood there fussing.

Stacy stirred sugar into the lemonade. "Want a taste?" she asked.

Grandpa came over. "Sure do," he said and sipped a little.

Then he frowned and thought about it. "Well, I don't know. Give me a little more."

Stacy poured more lemonade.

Grandpa drank all of it.

Then he thought and frowned. "I think it's still too sour."

Stacy added a pinch more sugar. "Here. Now try it."

Grandpa held out his glass. "Give me plenty," he said.

Then Stacy began to giggle. "You don't fool me, Grandpa. Why didn't you ask for a full glass to start with?"

Grandpa chuckled and winked at her.

"My friends are dying of thirst," Stacy said. "I'd better get back outside." She carefully carried the tall pitcher.

Granny passed her on the garden path.

But Stacy didn't notice if Granny had made any purchases. She was too busy to look.

Stacy set the pitcher down on the sale table. The kids came running.

She poured one glass after another. Then she sat under the table and fanned herself. "Maybe it's just too hot for a yard sale."

"No way!" Dee Dee said. "It's a totally cool idea!"

"Yep," said Jason. "And we just made some bucks."

Stacy couldn't believe it. "We did?"

Dunkum filled her in. "Your granny bought several things. She's a big spender."

Stacy laughed. "Let me guess," she said. "A half pair of pj's?"

"You got it," Eric chimed in. "And some smelly cologne, too."

"Anything else?" asked Stacy.

Eric was smiling. "I bought your angel doll. For fifty cents!" He pushed the angel into his pocket. Its halo stuck out. "Do you think Abby will like it?"

Stacy gulped. "Did you say 'Abby'?" she squeaked.

"Yeah. It's gonna be her birthday present from me," Eric said.

"You're giving my angel to *Abby*?" said Stacy.

Eric nodded his head. "Tomorrow, when she gets back from camping," he said.

Dee Dee wrinkled her nose and stared at Stacy.

Stacy looked at Dee Dee and made another gulp.

They'd sold the present Abby had given to *her*. And Eric was using it for *Abby's* birthday gift!

*I have to get it back*, she thought.

But how?

# Seven

It was suppertime. The kids went home to eat. They left the yard sale table all alone.

"See you," Jason shouted.

"Bye," said Stacy.

"Have a good supper," Eric called.

The angel stuck out of his pocket.

*What'll I do?* Stacy worried.

Then her mother called, "Ready to eat?"

"I'm coming," Stacy said. She dragged her feet into the house.

She smelled fried chicken. But she didn't feel hungry.

*Sniff.* Something else smelled good.

Granny grinned. "Such a nice backyard sale," she said.

"Glad you liked it," Stacy told her.

Grandpa winked. He smelled just like the yard-sale cologne.

Stacy wondered about the pajama top. But she didn't say a single word.

Poor Grandpa. Now he'd have to wear his pj top for sure.

Stacy thought and thought. Wearing pajama tops or bottoms wasn't a problem. But something else was.

Eric was going to give Abby the angel. *That* was a problem. A *big* one.

*I have to stop him*, Stacy decided.

Determined, she gave him a call.

"I need my angel back," she said.

"Why?" Eric asked.

"I shouldn't have sold it," she said. "That's why."

"Well, you did. And now I have to eat supper," he said.

Eric hung up.

Stacy wanted to run across the street. Right to his house—right this minute!

■■■

After supper, Stacy took an old sheet outside. She wanted to cover up the sale stuff.

She wanted to make sure everything was safe.

But something seemed strange.

She looked all around the table. "This is weird," she whispered to herself.

The table seemed empty. *Very* empty.

She thought of all the cool sale items. Dunkum's and Eric's things. Dee Dee's stuff.

"Where *is* everything?" she said out loud.

Then she glanced around, feeling worried. Had a thief come during supper?

Carefully, she inspected the table.

Two of Dunkum's baseball gloves were missing. So was his radio.

Dee Dee's cat collar was gone. The bee stuffed animal and guitar books were missing. And a bunch of other things.

"I don't remember selling any of those," she said.

Stacy searched everywhere.

*Where could they be?* she wondered.

Then an idea struck.

Maybe the kids had taken some of the things home for safekeeping. Maybe *that's* what had happened.

Stacy thought hard.

Nope, the kids wouldn't do that. Not without telling her.

So Granny was the one to talk to. Maybe *she* had bought all those things.

Maybe . . .

Stacy checked around for the money box. Gone.

*Dunkum probably has it.* He was in charge of the club fund.

She hurried back inside.

"We're ready for dessert," said her mother.

"Where's Granny?" Stacy asked.

"Down the hall," her mother said.

Stacy found Granny in the bedroom. She asked about the missing sale items.

"I bought two things," Granny said. She held up two fingers. "Nothing else."

Stacy didn't need to be told what they were.

"Are we ready for dessert?" her mother called.

Stacy hurried back to the kitchen. She picked up the phone. "First, I have to call Dunkum," she said. "It's very important."

Grandpa chuckled. "What's more important than strawberry shortcake?" he teased.

"A backyard bandit," Stacy said. "I think someone's stealing our sale stuff."

Grandpa scratched his head. "What a horrible thing. Can't kids have any fun these days?"

"I'm going to find out what happened," Stacy told him.

He got up and peered out the back door. "Who'd want to do such a thing?"

"That's what *I* want to know," Stacy said.

She punched in the phone number.

Dunkum answered. "Hello?"

"Hi, it's Stacy. I think someone's ripping us off!" She explained about the missing things.

"Maybe you should do some spying," he suggested. "Maybe the thief will come back."

"Good idea!" she said. "I'll spy tonight . . . after dark."

"Be careful," Dunkum warned.

"I will," she said. "I promise."

Stacy hung up and ate her dessert.

Then she headed outside.

But she could only think of one thing. The cloth angel doll. A gift from her very best friend.

# Eight

The moon was full. Too bright for spying. Stacy crept outside anyway.

She found an empty trash can. But it was too far from the sale table. So she dragged it across the backyard.

*Good idea*, she thought. And she crawled inside the smelly garbage can.

For a few minutes, she pinched her nose shut. But breathing through her mouth was horrible.

*Who knows what might fly in!* she thought. *Or what might be creeping by my feet.*

Wicked worms and bugs and things. All of them might be crawling inside the trash can.

*Icksville!* Stacy shivered.

She let her nose do the breathing.

But . . .

*Pee-yew!* What an awful smell.

Quickly, she lifted the lid for some fresh air.

When she did, she saw two shadows. Kid-sized ones.

Who were they?

Stacy inched the lid off the trash can. She leaned forward and listened.

The shadows were whispering.

Were they inspecting the sale stuff? Plotting to steal?

She perked up her ears. The voices were familiar. And they were discussing something.

Stacy listened hard as she watched.

"I'll trade my parrot for your leather coin case," a voice said.

It was a tiny voice. Dee Dee Winters' voice!

Had Stacy heard right? Did Dee Dee want to *trade* something?

Stacy couldn't believe her ears.

Now the boy-shaped shadow was talking. It sounded like Eric Hagel.

Stacy couldn't hear everything he was saying. But it was about Dee Dee's stuffed animal. Her parrot—all blue, green, and orange.

*What's going on?* Stacy wondered.

She watched closely.

Now Dee Dee was holding her cat up to the table. "Did you ever see such a cool backyard sale?" she said.

*Mew*, replied Mister Whiskers.

Dee Dee giggled. "You know a good sale when you see it," she said.

Eric laughed. He held up his hamster. "Fran the Ham says there oughta be free lettuce to munch." He made his voice twitter like a hamster's.

Dee Dee and Eric went on talking back and forth, pretending.

At last, Eric spoke in his regular voice. "Won't our flags look great for Flag Day?" he said.

"Stacy's idea was real cool," Dee Dee answered.

Stacy felt a kink in her leg. She tried to stretch inside the trash can.

*I have to get out of here*, she decided.

But . . .

She leaned too far forward.

*Bang-a clank!*

The trash can fell over, and Stacy tumbled out.

Eric and Dee Dee screamed and ran away.

*Rats!* "So much for spying," Stacy muttered as she got to her feet.

She stood there alone in the moonlight.

She brushed herself off. No more icky insects crawling on her!

Silently, she ran to the house.

She felt terribly upset. And she smelled like a trash heap. So she took a bath and went to bed.

Later, in the darkness, she reached for her cloth angel.

Then she remembered. . . .

It was gone.

Sold to Eric for fifty cents!

# Nine

**I**t was Sunday morning. Church day.

But Stacy's thoughts were somewhere else.

"I have to talk to Eric before Sunday school," she told her dog. Sunday Funnies had already found the newspaper. And the comics.

She hurried to the teeny-weeny attic window. She pushed her face against it. "Can't see a thing," she muttered.

So she combed her hair and got dressed.

Before anyone else was up, she went outside. She dashed across the street.

*Brr-i-i-n-g!*

She gave the doorbell one long ring.

Eric just *had* to answer it.

She waited.

And waited.

At last, he opened the door. "What are you doing over here?" he asked.

Stacy stared at him. Blond hairs stuck out every which way!

"I came for my angel doll," she said.

He raised his eyebrows. "It's mine. I already told you."

"I know, but I want it back," she said.

Eric frowned. "I paid for it, Stacy. It was on the sale table!"

Stacy shook her head. "Well, I never should've put it there."

"But you did." Eric bunched up his mouth.

"I *have* to have it back!" she shouted. Stacy crossed her arms and made a big frown. She tapped her toe and waited.

Surely, Eric would come to his senses.

"I said it's mine," Eric grouched.

Stacy could not believe her ears. "You'll be sorry, Eric Hagel," she said. And marched home.

■ ■ ■

After church, Stacy saw Eric again. He was standing outside, waiting for his mother.

"Did you listen to the preacher today?" she asked.

"Uh-huh," he answered.

"Well? Are you going to be a cheerful giver?" she asked.

Eric stared at her. "Are *you* going to be a grumpy giver?"

Stacy didn't answer. Eric was right about her, but it still didn't sound so nice.

Then she remembered the missing sale stuff. "Have you heard about the robbery? I think there's a bandit in our cul-de-sac," she said.

Eric scratched his head. "What are you talking about?"

She told him. "Lots of our sale stuff has disappeared."

"Since when?" he asked.

"Last night, during supper. That's when the robber must have come," she explained.

He shook his head. "Don't know anything," he said.

"Some of *your* stuff is gone, too," she said.

Eric's eyes got big. "My stuff? Don't you mean the stuff I *donated*? I'm no grumpy giver," he insisted.

"Very funny, Eric," she said.

And Stacy spun away on her heels.

# Ten

Stacy looked at her watch.

Almost two o'clock.

Eric was being a big pain. He refused to give back the angel no matter how many times she asked.

Stacy felt horrible.

Abby Hunter would be home soon. Very soon.

Stacy didn't know what to do. She couldn't get Eric to budge.

Besides that, there was a mystery to solve.

Who *was* the backyard bandit?

Stacy had no clue.

She raced down the cul-de-sac to Dee Dee's house. "We have a problem," she said when Dee Dee opened the door.

Dee Dee let her in. "What's wrong?"

"There's a bandit on the loose," Stacy said.

"A what?" Dee Dee's eyes were wide.

"Lots of our sale stuff is missing," she explained.

"Oh, that." Dee Dee grinned.

Stacy stared at her. "Do *you* know who the bandit is?" she asked.

"Follow me," Dee Dee said.

They went upstairs.

"Is this what you're missing?" Dee Dee asked.

There was Dunkum's old radio on the dresser.

"What's it doing here?" asked Stacy.

Dee Dee explained. "I traded some of my stuff with the boys."

Stacy couldn't believe her ears.

"How can we make any money *that* way?" she demanded.

"Oh, there's plenty of money," Dee Dee said.

"There is?" Stacy said, surprised.

"Sure! Your granny paid bunches of money. She bought that smelly old cologne. Your grandpa's pajama top, too," said Dee Dee.

"For how much?" Stacy asked.

"Twenty bucks," answered Dee Dee.

"*Twenty?* That's way too much!" said Stacy.

"I know, but she wouldn't listen," Dee Dee said.

Stacy couldn't believe her ears.

"Your granny wanted to make some nice kids happy," Dee Dee explained. "That's just what she said."

"Nobody told *me* about this," Stacy said.

Dee Dee shook her head. "I guess you were busy making lemonade."

Stacy thought about everything. "So, we'll buy the flags with Granny's money?"

Dee Dee grinned. "Yep."

"Wow," Stacy said.

"Real cool," Dee Dee added.

"I guess there's only one problem now," Stacy said.

Dee Dee looked up at her. "The angel doll?" she asked.

Stacy nodded. "I need to get it back. What can I do?"

"I have an idea," Dee Dee said. And she whispered in Stacy's ear.

Stacy listened carefully.

Then she said, "You're right. Thanks for a great idea!"

And up the street she ran—to see Eric about the angel.

■■■

When Stacy found Eric, he was playing with his hamster. A teeny-tiny cat collar was on Fran the Ham's neck.

"Nice trade," Stacy said. She meant the cat collar.

Eric looked up. "Oh, you heard?"

She nodded. "You traded your treasures. Want to trade something with me?" she asked.

"Whatcha got?" he said.

"A whole sale table full," she replied.

Eric smiled a strange little smile. "Really? You'd give me *everything* on the table?"

Stacy nodded. "Only if you give back my angel doll."

Eric rubbed his head. "You must really want it," he said.

"Sure do," she said.

"What's so special about it?" he asked.

She took a deep breath. "Abby gave it to me a long time ago."

Eric's eyes nearly popped out. "*Abby* gave it to you?"

"That's why," she said softly.

"Why didn't you tell me?" Eric said.

"I should have," Stacy replied. "I'm sorry."

Eric grinned at her. "This is our secret, OK?"

"Thanks," Stacy said.

"And you can forget about trading the sale stuff," he said. "I don't want it."

Stacy smiled. "You're a cheerful giver."

"Here, hold my hamster." Eric ran inside to get the angel.

Stacy held Fran the Ham carefully.

At that moment, Abby and her family rode up the cul-de-sac. The Hunter family waved to her.

Stacy called to them, "Welcome home!"

Abby leaned out the van window. "Did I miss anything?" she asked.

"You just wait," Stacy said, grinning.

Abby smiled back. "Double dabble good," she said. Then she unloaded two suitcases and ran to her house.

Fran the Ham made cute little sounds in Stacy's hand.

Stacy leaned down and whispered in her teeny-weeny ear. "Flag Day's gonna be super. Thanks to a super-duper Granny."

She thought for a second. "Thanks to Eric, too."

Stacy felt great. Even if she did say so herself.

# Tree House Trouble

To
Leslie Brinkley
(Smile!)

# One

**I**t was Arbor Day.

Abby Hunter tiptoed outside. She hid behind the backyard fence. She peeked through its wooden boards. She watched Stacy Henry and her grandpa dig a hole. They were planting a tree.

Abby leaned on the fence, wishing. Wishing and snooping . . . on her own best friend.

Suddenly, she had a nose tickle.

A *big* tickle.

Sneezing and snooping didn't mix.

She pinched her nose tight and held her breath. She counted to ten in her head.

At last, the tickle went away.

Now Abby could snoop some more. Stacy and her grandpa were laughing and talking.

They were having a double dabble good time.

Soon, Abby had another nose tickle. But she would *not* sneeze. She would not let the terrible tickle win.

She twisted her nose. First this way, then that way.

She pooched her lips.

She held her breath.

Even pinched her nose shut with both hands. Of course, she'd need to breathe again pretty soon.

*One quick breath*, she thought.

She breathed in and out. But the tickle was still there.

Before she could clamp her nose shut . . .

*Achoo!*

A sneeze escaped.

Stacy jumped. "Who's there?"

Abby tried to answer, but more tickles teased her nose.

*Arga-choo-o!*

There—at least her nose felt better. But phooey! Stacy had caught her snooping.

"Need a tissue?" Stacy asked. She was leaning over the fence now, staring.

Quickly, Abby stood up. She brushed off her jeans. "I'm OK, thanks."

Stacy frowned. "What are you doing in the dirt?"

"Watching . . . uh, spying, I guess you'd say."

Stacy laughed out loud. "Why spy? Just come on over."

Abby felt silly. Snooping was stupid.

"Want to help plant a tiny tree?" Stacy asked.

"Thought you'd never ask." Abby jumped over the fence.

*Ker-plop!* She landed on Stacy's side.

Of all the wonderful things God made, trees were tops. Abby liked trees. No . . . she *loved* them!

Tall trees, short trees.

Trees with flowers and trees without.

Trees with fat, wide branches. And trees with secret holes where squirrels hid nuts.

She especially liked climbing trees. They had sturdy branches close to the ground.

Stacy's grandpa grinned a welcome. "Hi there, Abby." He carried the sapling toward her. "We could use an extra pair of hands."

Abby smiled. "Glad to help."

She noticed the tree's root system and its graceful branches. Beautiful.

"Ever plant a tree?" Stacy asked her.

"Nope," Abby said. "But I've always wanted to." She helped dig the hole for the tree, deep as can be.

She and Stacy steadied the sapling. Stacy's grandpa began to fill the hole with dirt. Lots of dirt.

Together, Abby and Stacy tugged on the long water hose. They watered the new tree.

When that was done, Stacy's grandpa stepped back. He tilted his head. First one way, then the other.

At last, he grinned. His dimples showed. "Fine and dandy," he said.

Stacy copied her grandpa. She took three giant steps back. She had to see if the tree was straight.

Abby giggled and did the same. Both girls eyeballed the tree. "It's real pretty," Abby said.

"It'll be huge someday," Stacy replied. "Like the one over there." She pointed to the oak in the corner of the yard.

Grandpa wiped his face. "It'll take years for this sapling to grow full size."

"Our oak tree is big enough to live in, don't you think so?" Stacy asked Abby.

Abby stared up at the towering branches. They almost seemed to reach to heaven.

That's when her idea got started. A double dabble good idea.

"Let's build a tree house," she said.

Stacy's eyes shone. "Maybe Grandpa will help."

Abby looked up at the huge tree again. "I think we're going to need a lot of help."

"Some of the boys might want to pitch in," suggested Stacy.

Abby wasn't so sure. She felt a little selfish. "Let's think about it. Don't say anything to the Cul-de-Sac Kids yet."

"Why not?" Stacy asked.

"The tree house could be private," Abby whispered. "Just for you and me."

"You mean don't tell Eric or Dunkum? Or Dee Dee or Carly?" Stacy asked.

"Not my brothers, either. And especially not Jason," Abby said.

"You mean keep it a secret?" said Stacy.

"Wouldn't it be fun? *Our* secret?" Abby whispered.

Stacy finally agreed.

Abby could hardly wait to get started!

# Two

**A**bby headed for her own house.

She rushed into the garage. She borrowed two hammers and some long nails. She found two pairs of work gloves.

Her father was full of questions. "Are you making something?" he asked.

She glanced around. "A hideout," she whispered. "For Stacy and me."

Her father nodded. "Sounds like fun. Where?"

"In Stacy's backyard. But it's top secret," Abby said.

"What about your club motto?" he asked.

Abby didn't want to think about the motto.

Not today. Not when she and Stacy were having such fun, just the two of them.

"'The Cul-de-Sac Kids stick together,'" her father reminded her. He was frowning a little.

"What's wrong with one little secret?" she said. "Why can't we have a tree house for two?"

After all, she and the other kids on Blossom Hill Lane did everything together. Everything! Before school, after school. And, except for homework time, most of the times in between.

Two girls could build a tree house. They didn't have to share their plans, did they?

Besides, it wasn't really against club rules. Was it? She should know. She was president of the Cul-de-Sac Kids.

If they *were* breaking the rules, nobody would know. Nobody at all.

■■■

Stacy's grandpa was a big help. He was strong. Cheerful too. He found scrap pieces of wood. And odds and ends of lumber.

Stacy's granny helped, too. She agreed to

cover for the girls. She helped keep their secret when the doorbell rang.

Granny told them about it later. Jason and the other boys had dropped by. They were asking questions. Lots of them.

"We heard pounding," Jason had said.

"Where's Stacy . . . and Abby?" asked Dunkum.

Granny was double dabble good. She told them Stacy was busy. "And so is Abby," she said.

It was true. Granny would never lie.

But Eric wouldn't give up. He had to know if Abby was at Stacy's house.

Granny was so cool. She didn't let on. Not a single secret slipped out.

"Thanks, Granny," Stacy said. "You were terrific."

Next came a group hug.

"Hey, wait for me!" Grandpa hollered.

Abby and Stacy held out their arms. Grandpa squeezed into the hug. Now it was a *bear* hug!

Abby thought her ribs might pop.

Stacy squirmed and giggled.

When the hug was over, Abby giggled a

nervous laugh. "Our tree house is still top secret. Isn't it?"

"Sure is!" shouted Stacy.

But Abby was worried. *How long before the others find out?*

# Three

It was Saturday evening.

The tree house was finished. There were little wood slats for steps. A cute red roof on top. And plenty of room.

It was shaped like a box. A yellow one, high in the branches.

Abby and Stacy stared at their secret.

"We need stuff for our hideout," Abby said.

"You're right." Stacy ran to her house. She came back with her dog, Sunday Funnies. "Every tree house needs a pet," Stacy said.

Abby agreed. "I'll get something, too. Our hideout needs to be cozy."

She ran home to ask her mother for some old pillows. But Abby spoke softly so Shawn and Jimmy and Carly wouldn't hear.

"Must you whisper?" Mother asked.

Abby replied, "It's a secret."

"Oh, a *secret*. Well, okay," said Mother, smiling.

Abby flew out the back door with two pillows.

She glanced around for snoopers. Quickly, she jumped over the backyard fence. Then she climbed the tree. Not a single Cul-de-Sac Kid was in sight.

Stacy leaned out of the tree house. "Be careful," she called.

Abby did some fancy footwork. But she made it to the top. Inside, she arranged the pillows. "One for you. One for me."

"This is so much fun," Stacy squealed.

"Sh-h! We don't want anyone to hear us," Abby warned.

Stacy looked below. "Oops. I almost forgot."

They sat down in their tree house and grinned. "This is the coolest place on earth," Abby said.

"Sure is," said Stacy. Sunday Funnies snuggled against her.

"Did you bring some dog food along?" asked Abby.

Stacy shook her head. "Why? We aren't spending the night."

"It would be exciting," Abby said. "Do you want to?"

Stacy frowned. "Mom'll probably say no."

"Well," said Abby, "maybe we should ask."

"*You* ask," Stacy insisted. "It's your idea."

"OK!" Abby picked her way back down the tree.

Sleeping in a tree house was a double dabble good idea. Wasn't it?

■■■

"What did my mom say?" asked Stacy.

Abby pulled herself back into the tree house. She plopped down on her pillow and smiled. The wind blew through her hair.

"C'mon, tell me! What did she say?" Stacy asked again.

Abby crossed her legs. She grinned a sneaky smile. "You're allowed."

Stacy's eyes grew wide. "You're kidding! I can sleep outside? In the tree house?"

Abby could hardly believe it, either.

"How'd you do it? How'd you get my mom to say yes?"

"She said you could if *I* could," Abby explained.

"Really?" Stacy said.

"Your mom called my mom already," said Abby.

Stacy's mouth flew open. "Are you sure?"

"I'm *not* kidding," Abby answered. "But there is one problem." She paused for a second. "I forgot to tell her the tree house is a secret."

"Oh . . . no." Stacy groaned. "We'll probably be getting some visitors. Sooner or later."

"I know," Abby said. She felt rotten.

"We should have left things the way they were. Did we really have to sleep out here tonight?" Stacy said.

"Yes, we *really* did," Abby said.

Stacy glanced around. "Well, so far, so good."

"I don't see anyone," Abby added.

Stacy started to laugh. "We oughta have a watchdog. Sunday Funnies is the perfect choice."

Abby chuckled. "*That* ball of fluff?"

"You might be surprised," Stacy said. "My dog is amazing. Remember, he can smell the funny papers from three rooms away."

"But can he smell Jason or Dunkum?" Abby argued.

"Sunday Funnies can smell any Cul-de-Sac Kid!" Stacy replied.

Abby kept her mouth shut. She wasn't going to ruin things, not when they were up here. Up high was the very best place to be.

"Let's plan our sleep-over," Abby said.

"OK," said Stacy. "We each need a sleeping bag."

"And a lantern," said Abby.

Stacy frowned. "Don't you mean a flashlight?"

"Oh, you're right. I've been reading too many prairie stories," said Abby.

Stacy nodded. "We each need a flashlight."

"We'll read scary stories out loud," Abby suggested.

Stacy shook her head. "Nothing scary. I'd rather tell secrets till we fall asleep." Stacy leaned her head against her puppy.

"Do you really think we'll get any sleep?" Abby laughed.

"There's Sunday school tomorrow," Stacy said. "What if we fall asleep in church?"

"We won't," Abby said.

"Hope not," Stacy replied.

Abby wasn't worried about losing sleep. Or being tired at church. She was thinking about something else. How long before they'd have to share their secret?

She looked around. Their hideout was the best. It had little windows cut into the sides. And tiny flower boxes underneath.

"What are you thinking about?" asked Stacy.

"Nothing much," Abby said.

"Let me guess—"

"You probably could," Abby said. "Is it wrong to keep this place a secret?"

"The other Cul-de-Sac Kids will find out," Stacy answered. "You know they will."

"That's what I'm afraid of," said Abby. "Maybe it's time for a new club. A different club."

"What sort of club?" Stacy asked.

"A girls' club," Abby stated. "The Best Friends Club!"

Stacy was smiling. She seemed to like the idea. "Starting when?"

"Right now," Abby answered.

She fluffed her pillows. A bird chirped outside the little window.

That's when they heard the sneeze.

"Uh-oh. Someone's spying on us," whispered Stacy.

"Better not be," Abby whispered back.

But somebody was.

*Two* somebodies!

# Four

It was sunset.

"Don't move," Abby whispered. The girls hid under the tree house window.

Abby peeked out. She could only see shadows. "Sneezes come in threes," she whispered.

Stacy nodded. "I think you're right."

The girls waited and watched. One good sneeze deserved another. Especially in April when trees were budding. It was hay fever season.

Abby listened. It shouldn't be too hard to tell who was spying.

Then . . .

*Ah-h!* Abby's no-good nose tickle was back!

"Oh . . . don't *you* sneeze," Stacy pleaded.

Abby pinched her nose shut. "I'm trying not to." She held her breath.

But when she breathed, it sounded like *aah-gah*—

Stacy covered her puppy's ears.

*Choo-o-o!*

"We're toast," Stacy whispered.

Abby sneezed again.

From the ground, someone called, "Hey! Who's in that tree?" It sounded like Eric Hagel.

Abby grabbed Stacy's arm. They froze in place.

"I *know* someone's up there." This time it was Jason Birchall's voice.

The girls were silent as the sky.

Eric said, "Trees don't sneeze."

Abby almost giggled.

Then Jason made a weird sound. Like a frog or something.

That's when Sunday Funnies started barking. He wiggled away from Stacy. *Aarf! Aarf!* He leaned out over the tree house entrance.

"Oh, *this* is great. Now the boys know it's us," Abby said. She heard footsteps running away. Were the boys scared?

"Sunday Funnies is a true watchdog." Stacy sounded proud.

But Abby was upset. Stacy's dog had spoiled things. So had Abby's own sneeze!

"Where'd they go?" Stacy asked.

"Who knows," Abby replied.

Stacy sighed. "Sorry about my dog's big mouth."

"Don't say sorry. *I* was the one who sneezed." The girls grew quiet.

Then Stacy spoke up. "At least we kept our tree house secret for a while."

"Only one hour." Abby felt sad, too.

Before Abby could say Jack Sprat, the boys returned.

No sneezes now. Eric and Jason had brought flashlights. Giant-sized ones!

Abby ducked her head. "Lie down," she told Stacy.

But Sunday Funnies was too excited. He barked and barked.

Beams from the flashlights moved across the tree. Back and forth.

"Wow! Check it out," Jason said below. "That's a tree house and a half!"

"Stacy doesn't have a tree house," Eric insisted. "Does she?"

"Well, I'm not dreaming. Am I?" Jason laughed. "Let's have a closer look."

Abby bit her lip. What could they do?

Stacy whispered, "I think they're coming up."

Abby's heart sank. Their secret was history!

# Five

"Private property!" shouted Abby.

Eric and Jason stopped in their tracks. "Says who?" Jason hollered. He was halfway to the tree.

Stacy stood up, hugging her puppy. "You're not invited," she said.

"And we're not kidding," Abby spouted.

Eric frowned. "How come? It's just us— Jason and me."

"We're *not* blind," Abby snapped. "We know who you are."

Jason shouted, "What's your problem, Abby Hunter?"

"Nothing," she said.

Eric tugged on Jason's shirt. "C'mon. Looks like a private tea party to me."

Abby felt funny. "Sorry, boys. We . . . uh . . . started a new club," she explained.

Jason and Eric were standing at the base of the tree. Their flashlights were still shining.

"What happened to the Cul-de-Sac Kids club?" asked Eric.

"Yeah, what about *us*?" Jason said.

Abby swallowed hard. She didn't know what to say.

"We're having a sleep-over tonight," Stacy offered. "Just us girls."

Eric flicked off his flashlight. "C'mon, Jason, let's go."

Then Jason began to sing. "Nanny, nanny, boo-boo. We'll just have to sue you."

"Don't be silly," Abby spoke up. "You can't sue us for having a sleep-over."

"We'll see what the *other* Cul-de-Sac Kids say," Jason said.

"Yeah, we'll just see," said Eric.

Now Abby was worried.

But . . . wait. *She* was the president. The Cul-de-Sac Kids couldn't do anything without her. Could they?

"Jason! Come back here," she called. "Don't cause trouble for the club."

"*Me* . . . cause trouble? Who're you kidding?" He turned and laughed, then ran for the garden gate.

Stacy started to climb down the tree.

"Where are you going?" Abby said.

"We need sleeping bags, right?" Stacy asked.

"Some snack food, too," Abby replied. She followed her friend down.

"Hurry back," Stacy called and ran to her house.

"I won't be long," Abby promised, heading home.

What else could go wrong?

## Six

**A**bby was coming out of her bedroom.

*Ka-poof!* She bumped into her sister in the hallway.

Carly stared at the sleeping bag. "What's that for?" she asked.

"It's for sleeping," said Abby.

"Outside?" asked Carly.

"Where else?" Abby replied.

"Mommy!" Carly wailed.

Abby shook her head. When would her sister grow up?

She hurried to the kitchen. The cookie jar was full. Double dabble good! She filled her backpack with goodies.

Two bags of crackers.

Some mild cheese.

Four napkins (just in case).

A thermos of milk.

Two drinking straws.

Four oatmeal cookies.

And two apples.

She hurried to the door. Her sleeping bag was rolled up in one arm. Her backpack in the other.

Now she was ready.

But someone was coming toward the kitchen. She heard fingers snapping. And humming.

It was Shawn! She was sure of it.

Where could she hide?

Not the pantry. Too skinny.

Under the sink? Too crowded.

Behind the refrigerator? Too heavy.

Think fast! Could she make it to the back door?

*Zip!*

She flew past the fridge, sink, and pantry.

*Whoosh!*

She was outside.

*Too close*, she thought.

Relieved, Abby headed for the garden gate.

*Squeak!* The screen door opened behind her.

"That you, Abby?" It was Jimmy.

She turned to see her little brother. He was hanging out the door.

"Oh, hi." She faced him the best she could, trying to hide her backpack, especially.

He stared at the sleeping bag. "Why you sleep outside?" he asked. His English was still jumbled up. Jimmy and his brother, Shawn, had been adopted last fall from Korea.

Abby looked at the sky. "It's a nice night. Don't you think so?"

Jimmy peered up. "Yes, very nice." It sounded like *velly* nice.

Abby didn't mind. She just wanted him to go back inside. But she didn't say that. He might get too curious. "When you're older, you'll sleep outside, too," she told him.

"I old *now!*" He came outside and stood tall. "Jimmy Hunter very old."

Abby laughed. "First graders are *not* old."

"Are too!" he insisted.

*Now what?* she wondered. She didn't want him to follow her. "Isn't Mom calling you?" she asked.

Jimmy cocked his head and listened. "Not hear mother."

"But you're hungry, right?" she tried again.

"I watch Abby put treats in bag." He pointed to her backpack.

*The snoop!*

"There's plenty more in the kitchen," she hinted.

Across the fence, Stacy was calling, "Abby! Hurry up!"

Abby felt trapped. "Time for bedtime snack," she told Jimmy. "Better go inside now."

But Jimmy was pushy. "I eat outside . . . with big sister."

He was being impossible.

"I have to get going," Abby said. "Maybe some other time."

*"Now!"* Jimmy stamped his foot. "Eat with sister now!"

Just then, Shawn showed up. So did Carly. "What's going on?" Carly asked.

"It's nothing," Abby said.

"Is *something!*" Jimmy shouted.

"Well, Mom said to come in," Carly bossed.

Abby kept quiet. She was tired of fussing.

Shawn spoke to Jimmy in Korean. Then they went inside.

But Carly stayed. "Where are you going, Abby?" she asked.

"To Stacy's."

"What for?" Carly asked.

"Mom knows, so it's okay," Abby said.

Carly squinted her eyes. "Why can't you tell *me*?"

"You don't need to know everything," said Abby.

"Better tell me!"

"I don't have to," Abby answered. "Good-bye." She hurried through the backyard gate. *Carly's such a pain*, she thought.

Abby was glad she had a best friend. And the new Best Friends Club!

She couldn't wait to get back to the tree house. The private clubhouse.

She dashed across Stacy's yard.

But . . .

*Plop!* She dropped her sleeping bag. It rolled down the slope. Abby reached for it, and the string came untied.

"What's taking so long?" Stacy asked. She

was high atop the tree in the wonderful tree house.

"Everything's going wrong," Abby muttered. She tied up her sleeping bag again.

"Did you see my sign?" Stacy leaned out of the tree house to point to something.

"What sign?" Abby turned to look.

"Down there," Stacy said. She was shining a flashlight.

Abby saw the sign. She read it aloud. "'No Boys Allowed.'"

"Like it?" Stacy asked.

"It's double dabble good!"

Abby dragged her sleeping bag across the yard. Then she began to climb the tree. Partway up, a tickle hit her nose!

"Oh no. Not again," Abby complained.

"What?" Stacy called down from the tree house.

"I have to sneeze," Abby said.

"Don't drop your sleeping bag," Stacy said.

Abby couldn't stop the sneeze. *Achoo!*

"Bless you" came a voice. A weird, froggy voice. It didn't sound like Stacy one bit.

"Oh, great," moaned Abby. "Guess who's back."

Stacy peeked out the tree house window. "Jason? What're you doing here?" she called to him.

"R-ribbit," Jason's froggy voice replied.

Abby kept climbing. Faster.

Jason teased. "Well, lookee there. Abby Hunter's playing Tarzan!"

*Whoosh!* Abby swung over to the tree house. She found Stacy's flashlight and turned it on.

Looking down, she saw Jason and Eric. They were standing at the bottom of the tree.

"You silly frog boy," she called to Jason.

Stacy agreed. "Hey, you're right. Jason does look like a frog. Especially at night." Stacy was laughing.

So was Abby. But the boys weren't.

Eric pointed to the sign. "What's this supposed to mean?"

Stacy smirked. "Exactly what it says."

Jason sneezed. Three times.

"God bless you," Abby repeated three times.

Eric spoke up. "Are you *really* starting up another club? Without the rest of us?"

"We haven't decided yet," Stacy said.

"Yes, we have," Abby replied. "Our club's already begun."

Jason chirped some froggy sounds. "We'll see about that," he said.

"We sure will," Eric added.

They left as quickly as they'd come.

"What was that all about?" Stacy asked Abby.

"I'm sure we'll find out," Abby said.

"Sooner or later," said Stacy.

Abby hoped it wouldn't be too soon. She was ready for a snack. And a cozy bed under the stars.

Without nose tickles.

# Seven

**I**t was past midnight.

Abby awoke with a tickle. A *foot* tickle!

She reached into her sleeping bag. Down . . . down . . . down. She scratched and scratched. Ah-h! Much better.

Soon she fell back to sleep.

Seconds later . . . another tickle. This time it was her elbow. She scratched it and snuggled down.

Then still another tickle troubled her. She must be dreaming. So she let the tickle go.

Soon, it *really* tickled. Like a bunch of cooties!

In her sleepy fog, Abby thought of cooties. They had tickled her little sister once. Cooties had ended up in Carly's hair.

Lice. That's what Mother had called them. *Yuck!* Abby shivered.

Now there were more tickles. Lots more. And Abby knew she wasn't dreaming! She had to scratch the tickles away.

Quickly, she crawled out of her sleeping bag. She started to scratch, but the tickles were moving. These were very weird tickles. They were tickles that crawled!

She hoped they weren't lice. She wanted to scream. But Stacy was sound asleep. She didn't want to wake up her friend.

Abby turned on her flashlight. She saw the reason for the tickles. They weren't lice. They were . . .

"Ants!" she hollered.

Stacy sat up and rubbed her eyes. "Wh-a-at?"

"Look! We've got ants!" Abby said. She pointed to the crawling little black dots.

Stacy leaped out of her sleeping bag. She did an ant dance. "This is worse than a bad dream," she said.

Ants walked the floor of the tree house. They crawled up the walls and all over the window-sill. They even dotted the girls' pillows.

They were everywhere!

"I'm getting out of here," Abby said. She picked up her sleeping bag and shook it.

Stacy did, too.

The girls looked around.

"We must have dropped food scraps," Abby said.

Stacy shined her flashlight to check. "But I don't see any scraps. Just icky black ants!"

The girls tossed their sleeping bags to the ground. They scurried down the tree. Their sleep-over was over.

"See you tomorrow," Stacy said. And she headed for her house.

"Bye!" Abby called and turned to go.

Suddenly, something caught her eye. A glass object—long and narrow. She went to the base of the tree. "An ant farm? What's it doing here?"

She noticed something strange. The ant farm had been tipped over.

"Who would do this?" she asked the darkness.

Then she knew.

Jason and Eric!

"Is this their idea of getting even?" Abby almost laughed. She was double dabble sure she was right. The boys were mad because they couldn't be in the new club. The Best Friends Club.

Silly boys. Their ant farm couldn't scare *her* away.

Nope! She knew what she must do.

Right away.

# Eight

Abby hosed down the tree house with Stacy's garden hose.

*Swoosh!* She sprayed everything in sight.

Things got a bit soggy, except her sleeping bag. She put it on Stacy's back porch.

It was a warm night. The tree house would dry out fast.

Abby shook her sleeping bag again. She turned it inside out. She checked every corner. Still a few more ants. A few *dozen*!

She flicked the stray ants off with her fingers one by one. Just like cooties. *Yuck!*

Finally, the ants were gone.

Abby climbed back up into the tree house. She felt the wood floor. Still damp. She'd wait a little longer.

Then she spied the patio pillows in her backyard. They were waterproof. She decided to borrow them, just for tonight.

Soon the pillows were laid out. She unrolled her sleeping bag on top of them. She would sleep in the tree house to guard the hideout. All by herself. Her very own tree house. At least for tonight.

■■■

When morning came, Abby peeked one eye open.

No more ants. All clear!

She rubbed her eyes and sat up.

*Flump!* Something soft tapped her head. She looked up. White strips of paper floated in through the window near her. "Someone was very busy last night. I think I know who."

A toilet paper tent hung over the tree house. Like a huge spider web!

Abby laughed. "Wait'll Stacy sees this."

She got up and climbed down the tree. Stepping back, she looked at the oak tree. Her eyes scanned the huge trunk.

Then she saw it! Someone had marked out

the word "boys" on Stacy's sign. Now it read *No Girls Allowed.*

Abby frowned. "Wait till Stacy sees *this*!"

Jason and Eric were acting like big babies. They had no right to spoil the sign!

She thought and thought. The boys were out very late last night.

Hm-m . . . She could get Jason and Eric in *big* trouble. All she'd have to do was tattle.

*Should I?* she wondered.

■ ■ ■

Abby stopped Stacy in the hall before Sunday school. "I think Jason and Eric decorated our tree house."

"I'm not surprised," Stacy said. "My mom saw it, too. But let's not tattle."

"Why not? They deserve it," Abby said.

"They deserve something else, too," Stacy replied.

"What?" asked Abby.

"I think you already know." Stacy turned to the classroom.

*What's she mean?* Abby wondered. She followed Stacy to Sunday school. The older Cul-de-Sac Kids were already sitting down.

Shawn, Abby's Korean brother, was grinning at her. So was Dunkum, the tallest boy on Blossom Hill Lane.

Jason and Eric were smiling, too.

Abby sat beside Stacy. "What's so funny?"

"Who knows. But we'd better be ready for anything," Stacy answered.

Just then, a folded note landed on Abby's lap. She opened it.

The note read

*Remember the CDS Kids' Motto?*

*The CDS Boys*

Abby handed the note to Stacy.

Stacy read it. "Looks like the boys are in this together."

Abby nodded. "No kidding."

Stacy pulled on her curls. "Shouldn't we share the tree house with them?"

Abby couldn't believe her ears. "Are you crazy?" she whispered. "No way!"

The teacher arrived. It was time to begin.

Stacy opened her Sunday school book.

She stared at the lesson. "Look at this." She showed Abby. "It's about sharing."

Abby wasn't surprised. She'd read verses like this before. She looked over at Jason and Eric. They were still smiling big smiles.

*Rats! They're grinning about the lesson,* thought Abby. Well, they could just keep smiling. She wouldn't give up the tree house. Not yet!

# Nine

It was after dinner. Abby dashed to the tree house.

Someone had removed all the toilet paper. *Probably Stacy's grandpa,* thought Abby. He had come to visit Stacy and her mom after church.

Soon, Shawn and Dunkum showed up. Eric and Jason, too.

"We're coming up! Ready or not!" Jason yelled.

"No way!" Abby shouted back. "Wrap me up in toilet paper if you want to. Cover me with black ants. I'm not giving up this tree house!"

Dunkum looked surprised. "Why not? The tree house is big enough for everyone."

Abby looked around her. Dunkum was right. The tree house *was* big. Still, she didn't want to share. "Stacy!" she called toward the house. "Stacy, come!"

Her friend ran out the back door. She stared at the boys. "What's going on now?" Stacy asked.

Jason spoke up. "We wanna have a meeting. In the tree house."

"But we *always* meet at Dunkum's," Stacy argued.

Jason didn't give up. "The tree house is better," he said. "And you know it!"

Stacy looked up at the old oak tree. "So . . . you like *my* tree house?" she said.

Abby held her breath. Stacy had called the tree house *hers*!

Shawn, Abby's adopted brother, piped up. "Please, Stacy? We have very short meeting. Yes?"

Stacy looked over at Abby. And Abby felt funny. *Real* funny.

"It's time for something different." Jason was getting pushy.

Abby glared at him. "Different? Like last night?"

"What are you talking about?" Jason shot back.

"We had unwelcome guests. Little black crawling guests," Stacy spoke up. "The opposite of uncles!"

There was a gleam in Jason's eye. "So you had interesting company, huh? Sorry about that."

Stacy groaned. "Those ants were everywhere, Jason Birchall! A nasty trick! And you are *not* sorry!"

Jason smirked. But not for long.

Abby spoke up. "Stacy and I need to have our meeting now." She wanted Stacy to climb up. She wanted to talk to her friend in private. In *their* tree house.

"It's time for *all* of us to meet," Dunkum insisted. "The Cul-de-Sac Kids stick together. Remember?"

Abby was tired of hearing about the motto. She wished she'd never made it up. "Too bad," she said. "Stacy and I are starting our private meeting. So scram!"

No one moved.

Jason frowned. He pushed up his glasses.

"You've had enough meetings, Abby. You guys had a sleep-over meeting last night."

"We're not guys. And, yep, we sure did," Abby said.

"See? You *are* having too many meetings!" Jason shouted.

Abby wouldn't argue. Not in front of the others. She looked at all of them. "Hey, where's Dee Dee?" she asked.

The kids turned to count one another.

"And what about Carly?" Stacy asked. "Where is *she*?"

"Carly and Dee Dee will show up sooner or later," Eric said.

"We can't meet without them," Stacy said.

"That is, *if* we were going to," Abby added.

"Don't forget little Jimmy," Dunkum reminded them. "He's missing, too."

Abby thought about her little brother. Was Jimmy still eating dinner? "Who's gonna get Carly and Dee Dee and Jimmy?" she asked.

She hoped all of them would search. Then she and Stacy could have some peace. And a club meeting—a Best Friends Club meeting.

Shawn nodded. "I go find little sister and brother." He jumped over the gate.

Jason ran to find Dee Dee.

But Eric and Dunkum stayed and didn't budge one inch.

Abby bit her lip. Things weren't working out.

Not the way she'd hoped.

# Ten

Abby sat like a princess, high in the tree house. Her legs trailed over the edge of the door. "Stacy and I *have* to talk," she insisted.

"So talk," Eric said. "We'll wait. We won't come charging up to your tree house. We promise."

Quickly, Stacy climbed up. She flew into the tree house.

"What should we do?" Abby whispered.

"About the Best Friends Club?" Stacy said.

"Can't we have *two* clubs?" Abby said.

"I don't know," Stacy answered softly.

Abby felt sad. Really sad. She looked around. The tree house was just right. It was perfect for two girls.

"Don't you want to be my best friend?" Abby asked.

"Of course I do," Stacy answered.

"Then . . . what about just you and me? Shouldn't we have the Best Friends Club anymore?" Abby held her breath.

Stacy looked away. "I want to be your best friend. But—"

"But what?" Abby said.

"We're *all* best friends," Stacy whispered. "Aren't we?"

Abby glanced down at the Cul-de-Sac Kids. Dee Dee and Carly were standing with the boys now. Jimmy too.

But nobody was smiling. Not the kids on the ground looking up. Not the girls in the tree house looking down.

Stacy bit her lip. "I miss my *other* best friends."

Abby knew who those friends were. She wondered about the tree house. Nine kids was a lot for one hideout. How crowded would it be?

She thought some more. Sharing was a good thing. A double dabble good thing. The Sunday school teacher said so. So did the Bible.

Still, Abby was stubborn. She cupped her hands over her mouth. "I'm president of the Cul-de-Sac Kids!" she shouted.

The kids on the ground listened, their eyes wide.

"I'm going to say something. Something important," Abby said.

Now the kids looked eager. Dunkum and Jason were smiling.

"We are *not* having a meeting today. Everyone can just go home," Abby said.

Faces sagged. Especially Eric's. He looked mad.

"No Cul-de-Sac Kids meeting today," Abby repeated.

Stacy touched her arm. "Why not?" she whispered.

Abby shook her head. "Tell them it's *our* tree house. Just ours. Please?"

"I'm sorry, Abby. I can't." Stacy got up and climbed down the tree.

Abby watched her go. She wanted to cry.

Below the tree house, eight kids made a huddle. Abby couldn't hear what they were saying. She didn't want to.

In a few minutes, the kids headed for the

gate. Stacy too. They were laughing and talking.

Jason called over his shoulder, "Have a nice *private* meeting, Miss President." He chuckled.

Abby wished he'd bite his tongue. She also wished just one person would have said good-bye.

# Eleven

**M**onday morning. Time for recess! Abby ran to the swings.

"Did you hear the news?" Dee Dee Winters asked.

Abby leaned against the swing. "Nope."

Dee Dee couldn't wait to tell. "We've got a new club president," she blabbed.

"You do?" Abby couldn't believe her ears.

Dee Dee was grinning. "It's Stacy Henry."

Abby was stunned. "When did this happen?"

"Last night," Dee Dee said.

Abby wondered how that could be. The past president had to be voted out first. Didn't she?

Dee Dee kept talking. "We got ourselves a cool president. Really cool."

Abby didn't want to hear more. She ran toward the soccer field. "Everybody hates me," she sobbed.

■■■

After school, the Cul-de-Sac Kids walked home together. All but Abby.

Abby wanted to join them. But she didn't.

She thought about her best friend. *Stacy probably is a cool president, just like Dee Dee says.*

She looked both ways at the street. But she tried not to look straight ahead. The other Cul-de-Sac Kids were laughing. They were talking about the school day. She heard bits and pieces. . . .

Dunkum said he wanted to plant a fruit tree. "For Arbor Day," he said. "Like Stacy did."

"Better late than never," Stacy said.

Eric agreed and offered to help.

Dee Dee and Carly giggled and said they'd dig the hole.

Jason wanted to taste the first ripe fruit.

Shawn said he'd help him. And Jimmy would hang upside down from the tree.

But nobody said a word about Abby. Nothing.

"What about today's club meeting?" Dunkum said. He was walking next to Stacy.

"Want to use my tree house?" Stacy asked.

"Yes!" Dee Dee shouted. "I love tree house meetings."

"We're having a meeting?" Carly said.

"Can I bring my frog?" Jason asked. He did a jig on the sidewalk. He croaked, "Ribbit!"

The kids were laughing. Even Abby laughed before she caught herself. But no one heard her.

No one seemed to care.

Not even Stacy.

# Twelve

Abby felt left out. *Really* left out.

But it was her own fault and she knew it.

She decided to do a little spying. It couldn't hurt anything. Could it?

She went to Stacy's backyard gate. Leaning down, she peeked through the boards. The Cul-de-Sac Kids were perched high in the tree house.

She watched them closely. They were having a club meeting. Without her! There in the tree house with that fancy red roof. And those darling little windows.

She twisted the ends of her hair. The kids were saying their motto like they always did.

A big lump bunched up in her throat. She

tried to swallow. But the lump wouldn't move.

She coughed. Still stuck.

She coughed again. No use.

Then she felt a familiar tickle. A nose tickle.

"I should have stayed inside," she muttered. Before she could hold her breath, the tickle grew.

It grew so big. It got so strong.

*Arga-choo-o!*

The sneeze blew open the yard gate.

The Cul-de-Sac Kids stared down at her.

"Bless you," Stacy said.

Abby tried to say, "Thank you." Instead, she sneezed again.

This time, Jason and Dunkum said, "God bless you."

On the third and loudest sneeze, all the girls chimed in. "God bless you, Abby!" Carly and Dee Dee were giggling.

Someone started chanting the club motto. Jason and Stacy got it going. "The Cul-de-Sac Kids stick together," they said. "The Cul-de-Sac Kids stick together."

They kept saying it over and over.

When they stopped, Abby saw the new sign. *No Snobs Allowed*, the words spelled out.

Abby's nose tickle was gone. But her throat lump was back.

She swallowed hard. She wanted to talk to her friends. All *eight* of them. She wanted to tell them she wasn't a snob.

"I'm sorry," Abby blurted. "I was so selfish."

"You sure were!" Jason hollered.

"Hey, nobody's perfect," Carly said.

Stacy smiled but didn't say a word.

Eric waved at Abby. "Come up here! You gotta check out this tree house. It's the coolest place around."

Abby didn't say what she was thinking. *The coolest place is where my friends are,* she thought.

She climbed up the tree. She looked at her friends and took a deep breath. "The Cul-de-Sac Kids stick together," she said.

Everyone was clapping.

Jason was jigging.

Abby squeezed in next to Stacy. "Are you really the new president?"

"Just till *you* came back," said Stacy.

"Oh," Abby said, smiling. "I get it."

"Look how much room there is," Dunkum said.

"Oodles," Abby replied. And she meant it.

"It's a double dabble good tree house!" shouted Jason.

"Definitely," Abby said with a smile.

# BOOK 17

# The Creepy Sleep-Over

For
Peggy Littleton's first grade class
at
Colorado Springs Christian
Elementary School

Patrick Antrim
Brooke Humphreys
Julia Bennett
Kirsten Kruger
Matthew Fenlason
Amanda Lenehan
Adam Fekula
Cole Moberly
Conner Fitzgerald
Christopher Murphy
Brynden Flick

Luke Nelson
Rebecca Glisan
Chelsea Samelson
Eric Goldberg
Marielle Sheppel
Mark Hernandez
P.Y. Young
Carisa Hoogenboom
Blake Wittenberg
Jessica Hollingsworth
Aide: Sue Obenauf

# One

It was a super Saturday.

Dunkum Mifflin was jumping happy. He slam-dunked his basketball three times in a row. *Hooray!*

His name was on Miss Hershey's reading list. He'd checked it twice. He'd made his reading goal. Twenty-five books in all!

The reward was a sleep-over at the teacher's house. Eight kids from Miss Hershey's class were going, including Eric and Jason.

They'd eat pizza and junk food. And ice-cream sundaes and root-beer floats.

Best of all, they were spending the night!

Eric Hagel and Jason Birchall arrived at Dunkum's house. They passed the ball around. They talked about the sleep-over.

"Where's Miss Hershey's house, anyway?" Dunkum asked.

Jason didn't know exactly.

Eric didn't, either. "She used to be on my paper route. But not anymore," he said.

"Did she move?" Dunkum asked.

Eric scratched his head. "Guess so."

"Somewhere out in the country," Jason piped up. "I heard it's a haunted mansion!"

"How do you know?" Dunkum asked.

Eric and Jason laughed. "Everyone says so," replied Eric.

"*Everyone?*" Dunkum repeated.

"Well, you know." Jason crossed his eyes. "It's gonna be such a cool sleep-over. Even if the house *is* haunted."

Eric agreed. "I still can't believe it. Did I really read all those books?"

Jason grinned. "Your name's on Miss Hershey's list, right?"

Eric nodded and passed the ball to Dunkum.

Dunkum shot up ... up ... *Whoosh!* "Anyone else going from our cul-de-sac?"

"Abby and Stacy are," Eric replied.

"Abby oughta be going. She read over *fifty* books," Jason said.

"Wow! How'd she do it?" Dunkum asked.

"She's a bookworm. That's how." Eric laughed.

Dunkum was thrilled. Most of his friends were going to the sleep-over.

"I heard Miss Hershey tells bedtime stories," Eric said. "Spooky ones."

"Yeah, better watch out," Jason warned.

"How come?" Dunkum asked.

"She likes stuff by Edgar Allan Poe," said Eric. "Every year, same thing."

"Who's this Poe dude?" asked Dunkum.

Jason started laughing. "Edgar Allan Poe wrote mystery stories and poems. Ever hear of 'The Raven'? It's famous."

"Nope," Dunkum said.

"Well, you'll hear it plenty," Eric said.

Jason flapped his arms. "Sounds wingydingy. Get it? Ravens have wings—"

"Aw . . . Jason, act your age," Dunkum scolded.

"Whatever," Jason muttered and stopped flying around.

The boys shot some more baskets. "How do *you* know about the sleep-over?" Dunkum asked Eric.

"Miss Hershey has one every year. The kids from last year's class told me." Eric's voice was low and quiet. "They told me *all* about it."

Dunkum hoped the sleep-over wasn't too scary. He wasn't a scaredy-cat or anything. He just didn't like creepy things.

Jason interrupted his thoughts. "You're not afraid of haunted mansions, are you?" He made his voice sound spooky. "Ooow!" he squealed.

"You don't scare me!" Dunkum said.

"But Miss Hershey will," teased Jason.

Dunkum dribbled the ball hard. He leaped up and dunked it. That's how he got his nickname—Dunkum. His real name was Edward. But nobody called him that. He was Dunkum—the tallest and best hoop shooter around.

Dunkum thought hard as he aimed the basketball. Jason could say all he wanted. But their teacher was the best. She wouldn't plan a creepy sleep-over. No way.

Dunkum didn't believe it for one second!

# Two

It was Friday morning.

Heavy snow was falling. First storm of the new year.

Miss Hershey's class was all bunched up. Their teeth chattered as they huddled near the outside door.

Dunkum was glad for his heavy jacket. "Tonight's the sleep-over at Miss Hershey's house," he said.

"Maybe we'll get snowed in," Jason said.

Abby grinned. "I wouldn't mind. I heard about Miss Hershey's old house," she said. "She has eight cats. And she likes Mozart—especially songs in a minor key. Perfect for a haunted mansion, you know."

*Sounds like a haunted cat shelter*, thought Dunkum.

The first bell rang. Miss Hershey's classroom door swung open. She greeted the students. "Hurry, children. Come in where it's warm."

Dunkum liked her cheerful voice. She was saying things his mom might say on a cold day. He watched her smiling face.

She was cool. Really cool! Miss Hershey couldn't possibly live in a haunted mansion. Could she?

■■■

The teacher wrote the date on the board. *January 19*.

"Today is a famous person's birthday," she said. "Does anyone know whose?"

Abby Hunter raised her hand.

"Yes, Abby?"

"It's Edgar Allan Poe's birthday. He was born in 1809," Abby recited.

Dunkum's hand shot up.

"Yes, Dunkum?" said Miss Hershey.

"Poe was a *mystery* writer." Dunkum grinned. He was glad Eric and Jason had filled him in earlier.

Miss Hershey nodded and smiled. "That's right. Poe was born more than two hundred years ago today."

Dunkum listened as Miss Hershey told about Edgar Allan Poe. "He was an American poet. A short story writer, too," she said.

Dunkum liked short stories. He'd even written a few himself.

"Poe's works are almost like music," said Miss Hershey.

Dunkum had never heard such a thing. He'd read tons of books. But he'd never found tunes hidden in the words or sentences.

He didn't get it. What did Miss Hershey mean?

■■■

By recess, the ground was covered with white. But the snow had stopped.

Some of the Cul-de-Sac Kids made a fort. Abby and Stacy helped pack down the snow.

Dunkum and Jason carried armfuls of white wet stuff.

Eric and Shawn made little cannonballs out of snow.

Dunkum kept thinking about Miss Hershey's

house. "Why does she live in a mansion?" he asked Eric.

"She's weird, that's why," Eric said.

"How can you say that?" Dunkum replied.

"Well, she lives with a bunch of cats. No husband, no kids," Jason chimed in. "Isn't that kinda weird?"

"So what? Not everyone gets married," Eric said.

Dunkum knew that was true. His mother's cousin was almost forty and still single.

*Whoosh!* He plopped down a pile of snow near the fort. "Being single's not weird." Dunkum sighed. "I want to know why she lives in a mansion."

"Maybe she's rich," Abby spoke up.

Stacy shook her head. "I doubt it."

"How come?" Dunkum asked.

"Teachers don't make much money. Besides, she doesn't dress rich," Stacy said.

"No diamond rings or bracelets," added Abby.

Dunkum thought about that. "Miss Hershey dresses real pretty, though."

"And her hair's always perfect," Abby said.

"Maybe she gives her money away . . . to poor kids," Dunkum said.

"Hey! *I'm* poor." Jason laughed. He twirled his glasses around.

"Grow up," spouted Dunkum. "You're rich compared to some kids."

"Yeah, kids in India, for starters!" Abby said.

Dunkum gave Abby a high five.

Jason made a face and scooped up a handful of wet snow.

*Pow!*

He threw the snowball hard.

Dunkum dodged out of the way, laughing.

*Brr-i-i-ing!* The recess bell rang.

"What'll we do about the fort?" Dunkum asked. It was only half finished.

"We'll work on it later," Eric said.

The Cul-de-Sac Kids agreed and ran toward the school.

Dunkum didn't line up right away. He checked out the fort. It was really cool. It had a large main entrance, curved like a cave. There were lookout holes on the top and sides.

Making the fort with his friends gave him

a good feeling. Abby would call it double dabble good.

But he didn't feel so great about something else. Miss Hershey's house.

Was it *really* haunted?

# Three

**L**unch recess came fast.

The Cul-de-Sac Kids crawled around inside the snow fort. "This is better than making a snowman," Eric said. "And we've made lots of them."

Dunkum wasn't interested in a snowman. Something else was on his mind: the teacher's cats. "What's with Miss Hershey's cats? Why so many?" he asked.

Abby looked surprised. "She loves them, that's why."

"But eight cats? C'mon!" Dunkum answered.

"That's way too many," Eric agreed.

Jason was nodding his head. "I heard she willed her mansion to them."

"What's that mean?" Dunkum asked.

Abby spoke up. "When she dies, her cats get the house."

Dunkum couldn't believe his ears! He'd heard of fat cats, but *rich* cats?

Abby giggled. "They're like her children, I guess."

Dunkum shook his head. "Aren't *we* her children? Well, you know . . ."

Jason started jigging inside the snow fort. "Mamma Hershey . . . Mamma Hershey," he chanted.

The kids laughed, holding their stomachs. "You're crazy, Jason Birchall," shouted Eric.

Dunkum thought the same thing. Jason *was* a little crazy.

Finally, Stacy told Jason to quit dancing. "It's too crowded in here. Go outside and do your jig."

But Jason wouldn't listen. He kept it up. "Just wait till tonight," he said in a weird voice. "Miss Hershey's house will be as dark as midnight. There are no streetlights out there in the country. There'll be spooky music, too."

Eric joined in. "And don't forget all those cats." He and Jason were cackling like hens.

"Cats don't scare me," said Dunkum.

"What about *black* ones?" Jason joked. "How'd you like a sleep-over with eight black cats?"

Abby put a stop to it. "Nobody knows what color Miss Hershey's cats are. It doesn't really matter anyway."

"Abby's right," said Eric. "But what about the bathroom? What color is *that*?"

Eric, Abby, and Stacy started laughing again.

"Hey! What's so funny?" Dunkum asked. "Who says Miss Hershey even *has* a bathroom?"

"Yeah, who says?" Jason said.

Abby waved her hands. "Whoa! Miss Hershey's a human being. People need bathrooms, right?"

Eric's eyes were wide. "But she's our teacher, so that makes her special. And different."

Jason stopped jigging. "Then maybe she *does* have a bathroom and wears pajamas . . . and takes out the trash."

"Well, why not?" said Abby.

But Dunkum didn't want to hear about

Miss Hershey's pj's or her garbage. He wanted to know if her house was haunted. And how she discovered music in Poe's poetry.

■ ■ ■

Dunkum's mom helped him roll up his sleeping bag. They tied it neatly.

"Don't forget your toothbrush," his mother said. "And your warmest pj's."

Dunkum remembered his flashlight. He wanted to take it along for sure. "Anything else?" he asked.

His mother went down the teacher's checklist. "Let's see." Her finger slid over the page. "I think everything's packed now."

"It's just one night. I don't need much," Dunkum said.

His mother looked over the list again. "What about stuffed animals?" she asked. "It says you may bring two animals each."

Dunkum wondered about his friends. He'd heard Abby and Stacy talking. They were taking teddy bears. Two of the bears were going dressed as brides.

Dunkum had never seen a teddy bear in

a bride's gown. *Sounds like girl stuff*, he thought.

"I'm leaving my stuffed animals home," he said. Dunkum couldn't imagine Eric taking stuffed animals.

But Jason Birchall? Well, maybe . . .

Lately, Jason had gone pet crazy. He had a bunch of stuffed animals—snakes, lizards, and raccoons. Jason also had some strange real-life pets. Very strange.

Dunkum didn't want to think about Jason's bullfrog, or Jason's tarantula! Why did people keep so many pets, anyway?

The thought of Miss Hershey's eight cats bugged him again. But he pushed the pet thoughts aside. Nothing could spoil his reward. He had read twenty-five books and was going to his teacher's house!

Dunkum could almost taste the pizza, and the ice-cream sundaes. It was going to be a sleep-over to remember.

No matter what!

# Four

**M**iss Hershey's house sat high on a hill. It didn't look like a mansion. Not a castle, either. But it was big . . . and old. Like a fairy-tale house with a snowy roof.

"Wow!" Dunkum whispered.

His mother drove into the driveway.

Dunkum noticed tall trees along the road. And the icicles hanging from the porch. "What a cool place," he said.

"Sure is." His mom chuckled. "May *I* come to the sleep-over, too?" She was only teasing, of course.

*It's too pretty to be haunted*, Dunkum thought.

His eyes drifted over the area. A pair of stone lions caught his attention. They were statues, perched near the front door, one on each side.

"Hey! Look there," he said, pointing.

"Lions with full manes," his mother said. "I wonder where she bought them."

Dunkum stared at the lions. He didn't care about their manes or where his teacher had found them. He was looking at their mouths. They were closed!

*Good*, he thought. *These lions aren't scary*.

But it was daylight. Things always looked better in the light.

"You're going to have a great time," his mother said.

Dunkum waved good-bye. "See you tomorrow!"

■■■

"Welcome," Miss Hershey said at the door.

"Thank you," Dunkum replied. He glanced at the lion statues once more and went inside.

Abby and Stacy were there. They were sitting near a lamp with a fringe. Dunkum had never seen a lampshade like that. *Must be old*, he thought.

Jason and Eric were beside the hearth. The flames in the fireplace were snapping. Jason gave Dunkum a high five. "About time you showed up!" Jason said.

"The roads were a little slick," Dunkum replied.

Miss Hershey nodded her head and smiled. "You all arrived safely," she said. "I'm so glad."

Dunkum sat down with Jason and Eric. He had a good feeling about this sleep-over. A *really* good feeling!

■■■

Milo had *big* ears for a cat. He was black with yellow slits for eyes.

"Say 'hello,'" Miss Hershey said to Milo. He was perched on her lap. He only blinked occasionally. And he looked upset. Was that a frown on his kitty face?

Dunkum didn't know exactly. He didn't care much for cats. Rabbits were *his* thing.

Milo's eyes made Dunkum shiver. What a creepy cat! But Miss Hershey didn't seem to think so. She was hugging him and talking kitty talk. Or was it baby talk?

Dunkum couldn't be sure.

"Say 'hello' to the students," Miss Hershey told Milo again.

After many pleas and some kitty kisses, Milo spoke.

It sounded like *meow* to Dunkum. Nothing more.

Yet Miss Hershey kept fussing over Milo. What a spoiled cat!

"You're so-o-o wonderful, baby," she cooed.

Dunkum thought of his own pet, Blinkee. His poor bunny rabbit would not enjoy being around this many cats. Blinkee would have passed out by now, for sure!

Miss Hershey's pets turned out to be *four* cats. Not eight. Someone had stretched the truth times two.

So Milo had three little sisters. All fluffy black cats. They were Muffin, Minka, and Maggie Mae.

Muffin and Minka were OK names. But Dunkum wondered about Maggie Mae. Sounded to him like someone's great-aunt. A very strange name for a cat!

■■■

Miss Hershey served up hot pizza. Then she made sundaes for everyone: Hot fudge, caramel, and strawberry.

The cats were stuck with tuna delight.

Dunkum wanted both hot fudge *and* caramel topping. Abby and Stacy had strawberry topping, of course.

Eric asked for hot fudge. Jason, too, only he wasn't supposed to have chocolate. It made him jittery. He was having it anyway.

Dunkum glanced around. There were strange Old Mother Hubbard kitchen cupboards in a dark brown. The beamed ceiling was rusty brown. Same as the mantel over the fireplace. Even the hardwood floors were dull.

Dark wood. Black cats. Chocolate topping . . .

Was something scary inside those cupboards? What about the ceiling? Was something about to float down from the beams?

And the music? Abby was right about Mozart. Miss Hershey put on some violin music that sounded like a mystery waiting to happen.

Miss Hershey's cats were almost finished

with their dinner. They licked their chops, and Dunkum tried not to stare.

Milo stopped eating and glanced at Dunkum. Those orange-yellow eyes made him jumpy, and not in a happy way!

Dunkum turned around. He saw more goodies coming. Miss Hershey was bringing a tray to the table. "Care for a brownie?" she asked.

"Thank you." Dunkum took a medium-sized one. They were extra dark. Extra chocolaty, too.

After supper, Miss Hershey began to light candles. Lots of them! There were candles in the windows and on the long mantel. Tall candlesticks on the grand piano.

"Will you play something for us?" Abby asked.

"Yes! Play the piano," Eric begged.

All the kids chimed in. "Please?"

"Very well," Miss Hershey said. She went to sit down. But there were no music books in sight.

"How's she gonna play?" Jason asked.

"Maybe she plays by ear," Dunkum replied.

Jason laughed. "How's she gonna see where to put it?"

That got everyone going. Even Miss Hershey was chuckling.

When things were quiet, she began. At first, Dunkum thought the melody seemed a bit gloomy. But the more he listened, the more he liked it. Was it more Mozart?

Miss Hershey kept her hands on the piano keys as the last notes were still sounding. Slowly, they faded away.

Then she lifted her hands. The piece was done.

Before the kids could clap, she began to speak. Her words were soft. "I'd like to recite a poem from memory. It's one of my very favorites."

*Uh-oh*, thought Dunkum. *Is this the bedtime story?*

"'Once upon a midnight dreary,'" Miss Hershey began.

"It's from 'The Raven,'" whispered Abby.

Dunkum listened. He wouldn't let this raven poem shake him up. No way!

# Five

**M**iss Hershey continued. "'Suddenly there came a tapping, as of someone gently rapping, rapping at my chamber door.'"

The poem excited Dunkum. Was it the flow of the words? Was it the air of mystery?

He really didn't know, but he liked it.

Miss Hershey went on. There was a *visitor* tapping at someone's bedroom door. "'Only this and nothing more,'" said his teacher.

Suddenly, Dunkum felt something behind him. He froze. Someone was tapping on his back!

He turned to see.

It was Milo. He was pawing at Dunkum.

*Kung fu kitty*, Dunkum thought.

278

He almost laughed out loud, but he didn't move.

Milo kept it up.

*What's he want?* Dunkum wondered.

Miss Hershey was still saying the poem. "'Deep into that darkness peering . . .'"

It was hard to pay attention. Not when a cat was pounding his fat paw on Dunkum's back.

Was Milo trying to say something? Maybe he had to go potty.

Dunkum didn't know what to do. So he raised his hand like in school.

Miss Hershey stopped. "Yes, Dunkum?"

"Uh, I think your cat needs something," he said. "Milo's scratching my back."

Stacy and Abby giggled.

Miss Hershey nodded. "Oh, Milo's just being friendly. He likes you, Dunkum."

*Great*, thought Dunkum. *I don't like* him*!*

"Now, where was I?" Miss Hershey said. She faced the students. "Does anyone feel a beat, a rhythm in this poem?"

Abby and Jason raised their hands.

*What's she mean?* Dunkum wondered. He didn't feel any beats. He only felt tapping— from Miss Hershey's cat!

"Listen now," his teacher said. She continued.

Soon she came to a familiar part. Dunkum knew he'd heard it somewhere. ""Tis the wind and nothing more!'"

Milo continued his paw tapping. Dunkum wished the cat would back off! Be gone, with the wind, maybe?

When the poem was over, Dunkum raised his hand once more. "Sorry," he said when Miss Hershey called on him. "It's Milo again."

"Is he bothering you, Dunkum?"

"Can you make him stop tapping me?" asked Dunkum.

Miss Hershey began to smile, then laugh. "Oh, Milo. Dear Milo," she said. "You've finally found the beat."

"The beat?" Dunkum muttered. "He's beating on *me*!"

Eric and Jason were snickering.

But Miss Hershey explained. "Milo's heard 'The Raven' many times. More times than I can count." She went over and picked up her fat cat. "That's wonderful, kitty," she cooed.

Dunkum thought of the repeated sentences. *'Tis the wind and nothing more.* And

. . . *quoth the Raven, "Nevermore."* He felt a beat, too. Kinda. If Milo could feel it, maybe he should try, too.

Miss Hershey opened her poetry book. She gave it to Dunkum. "Here, you read it," she said.

He began. "'Once upon a midnight dreary, while I pondered, weak and weary . . .'"

Suddenly, he stopped. "Hey! I think I hear the beat," Dunkum said. "No, I can *feel* the beat!"

"That's very good." Miss Hershey seemed pleased.

But Dunkum had a question. "What does 'pondered' mean?"

His teacher explained. "To ponder means to think about something."

"Oh," said Dunkum. "I thought it meant to *pound* on someone!"

At that, Milo leaped toward Dunkum. The cat settled next to him.

Abby and Stacy giggled.

But Dunkum didn't laugh. He didn't know what to think. So he kept his eyes on Milo. And that swishy, bushy tail.

# Six

**M**iss Hershey finished her talk about Poe, the poet. Her bedtime story wasn't so bad. Wasn't scary at all. In fact, Dunkum thought it was interesting. Really interesting. He'd learned something new. He'd found the music in a poem. Well, at least he'd found the beat.

Later, Eric and Jason wanted to check out the old house. They had an important mission in mind.

Miss Hershey gave the OK. "This house is an exciting place," she told them. "Look around as much as you like."

She headed to the kitchen to make hot cocoa. The *deep* chocolate kind.

Abby, Stacy, and another girl stayed in the

living room. They were roasting marshmallows by the fire.

Two other classmates were playing board games.

Dunkum hurried to find Eric and Jason. They were upstairs, opening every door. "Hey! You guys are nosy!" Dunkum said.

Eric laughed. "We're just looking for the bathroom."

"I already told you. She probably doesn't have one," Dunkum insisted. "Remember, she's a *teacher*."

Jason jigged and jived.

"You had too much chocolate," Dunkum said.

"Wrong again!" Jason teased. "I need a bathroom."

Dunkum opened every door in the hallway. Even a broom closet.

Then . . . surprise! He found a walk-in closet.

He recognized certain clothes hanging there. "Look at this! I think I found Miss Hershey's closet."

Eric and Jason rushed over. "Let's see," said Eric.

"Any pj's?" Jason whispered.

"Are the clothes arranged from A to Z?" Eric teased.

"What about chalk? Or apples?" Jason said. "Maybe she stores her apples in there."

Dunkum turned around. "Stop it!" he said. He slammed the door behind him.

Jason frowned. "Wait! I was just getting started."

"I was afraid of that," Dunkum said. He shooed the boys back. "This is totally uncool. Miss Hershey oughta have some privacy."

Eric glanced at Jason. "Dunkum's right," he muttered.

But Jason dashed off. He darted here and there, looking for the bathroom.

Together they all searched. And found nothing.

Dunkum wasn't too surprised. "See? Told you!" he said. "Teachers don't have bathrooms!"

# Seven

**D**unkum and Miss Hershey blew out the candles in the living room.

Soon, the lights were turned back on. "Who wants to play hide-and-seek?" asked Miss Hershey.

Abby and Stacy looked surprised. "*Here?* In your house?" Abby said.

"Absolutely! You'll discover some wonderful places to hide," the teacher said.

Dunkum looked around.

*Uh-oh!* Jason was missing.

Eric waved his hand up. "Can I be It first?" he asked.

Stacy said, "Don't say 'can'—we know you can." She was always correcting speech. "You should say, 'May I be It first?'"

Eric shrugged like he didn't care. "Well? Can I?"

Miss Hershey agreed. "But you must count to one hundred very slowly."

"Why?" Eric asked.

"Because eight of us are hiding," she said.

"*You're* gonna hide?" Eric sputtered.

Dunkum was surprised, too.

"I love playing games," Miss Hershey said. "I'm still a kid way down deep." She chuckled.

For a moment, Dunkum believed her. He saw the wink of adventure in her eyes.

Just then, Jason came downstairs. He was grinning.

"We're going to play hide-and-seek," Miss Hershey told him.

"Yes!" Jason said. He looked right at Dunkum. "I know where *I'm* gonna hide!" And he disappeared again.

Eric began to count. "One . . . two . . . three . . . four . . ."

"Slow down," Miss Hershey said. "This is a very big house, you know."

Dunkum, Miss Hershey, and the others hurried to hide.

The sleep-over party was going great.
So far!

■■■

Dunkum ended up in the library. He found
a secret panel next to a set of encyclopedias.
He leaned against the wall.

*Squeak!* The panel door opened.

"Hey, cool," he whispered.

Quietly, he crept in. It was as dark as chocolate inside.

He sat on the floor and pulled the panel
door shut. "Eric will never find me here," he
said to himself.

He wondered if Miss Hershey knew about
the wall panel. What a secret, *secret* place!

Slowly, he counted to one hundred, just
like Eric was downstairs. Counting might
help to pass the time. Because he didn't want
to stay here too long. Not in this dark and
dreary place behind the library wall.

Suddenly, he thought of the Poe poem. Miss
Hershey's favorite. *Once upon a midnight
dreary . . .*

Shivering, Dunkum wished he hadn't remembered. Not the gloomy midnight part.

Not the raven part. This hiding place was way too creepy!

He waited a bit longer, listening. But he heard nothing. No sounds of Eric finding the others.

Maybe if he cracked the door, he'd hear better. Maybe even Eric's footsteps.

Dunkum listened longer.

Surely by now, Eric should be calling, "Coming, ready or not!"

Dunkum pulled on the panel door. It wouldn't move.

He pulled harder.

Stuck! It was honestly stuck.

Looking around was impossible. He couldn't even see his hand. And it was in front of his face! He knew it was because he bumped his own nose.

This time he jiggled the door. But it was jammed.

"Help!" Dunkum shouted. He called and called through the library wall, "I'm trapped! Somebody help me, please!"

# Eight

If Dunkum hadn't been so scared, he might've laughed. Here he was in the best hiding place of all.

Only *one* problem: It was too perfect. Hiding inside the wall meant Eric might never find him. Miss Hershey might not, either!

He kept calling.

He hollered.

He tried not to freak out.

If only Miss Hershey hadn't recited that raven poem. All of it seemed so spooky now. He wished he'd brought his flashlight up here.

Dunkum counted to one hundred again.

The waiting was getting boring. He yawned and leaned his head against the secret panel. He wished he were asleep in his own bed. . . .

■■■

Dunkum awoke with a start.

He heard pounding. "Dunkum? Are you in there?"

It was Miss Hershey!

"I can't open the door," he cried. "I'm stuck!"

"Don't worry, dear," his teacher said. "I'll get you out."

And she did.

*Click!*

The panel door opened, and Dunkum crawled out.

"You're the winner, Dunkum! You fooled *all* of us," said Miss Hershey.

"Hooray for Dunkum!" the kids shouted.

Abby and Jason were clapping.

"We thought we'd never find you," Eric said.

Dunkum was pleased. But he felt sorry, too. "I got a little carried away," he said.

Miss Hershey shook her head. "Oh no. Don't be sorry. I said this house was good

for hide-and-seek. But I didn't think it would swallow you up."

"It sure did," Jason piped up. He went to the wall and pushed the secret panel. He made it open and close. "Check it out! Why didn't *I* find this place?"

The others took turns with the wall panel.

Finally, their teacher said, "It's very late. Did everyone bring a sleeping bag?"

"And stuffed animals!" Abby said.

Dunkum wished now that he'd brought one. He followed the kids back downstairs. He whispered to Eric, "Did *you* bring a stuffed animal?"

"'Course I did," Eric said. "Didn't you?"

"I thought only the girls would," replied Dunkum.

Abby pinched up her nose. "Not really. You should see the stuffed animals Jason brought. He's got a lizard and a—"

"OK, OK," Jason interrupted. "Mind your own business, Abby!"

Dunkum wondered why Jason said that. Was he angry with Abby?

"It's almost midnight," Miss Hershey said. "Everyone's tired."

Dunkum wasn't. Not really. He'd snoozed for about half an hour inside the library wall.

"The living room will be the boys' bedroom," Miss Hershey told them. "Girls will sleep in the family room."

Dunkum rolled out his sleeping bag next to Jason. He found his toothbrush and flashlight. "Is there a bathroom after all?" he asked.

"Upstairs and three doors down," Jason said.

Dunkum remembered all those doors. "I thought that door led to a bedroom," he said.

"Nope, it leads to a huge bathroom," Jason said. He pushed up his glasses. "Yes, Dunkum, Miss Hershey *does* have a bathroom. She has three of them."

Dunkum nodded. "Guess that makes her a real human being, huh?"

"Three times over," Eric chimed in.

Dunkum wasn't surprised anymore. He'd learned some interesting things about his teacher. Miss Hershey was very cool. Even with cats!

Only cool teachers played hide-and-seek

with their students. And only the coolest teachers said they had a kid's heart inside.

Dunkum chuckled. He'd been so foolish. It was silly to think this house was haunted.

Really silly!

# Nine

The living room was dark now.

All the boys were sound asleep, except Dunkum. He was staring at the darkness. He couldn't get Poe's poem out of his head.

*Once upon a midnight dreary . . .*

He looked around the room. Eric was curled up in his sleeping bag. Two other boys were snoring. Jason was breathing loudly.

Just then, Dunkum thought he heard a sound. It wasn't a snore or a loud breath. It was something else.

He listened hard till his ears hurt.

*Whooooosh!*

Was it the wind?

Dunkum couldn't be sure. Part of him wanted to get up. *Go look out the window,* he thought. Another part wanted to hide inside his sleeping bag.

He started to sit up.

*Whooooosh!*

There it was again!

Dunkum's hands were shaky. He found his flashlight and flicked it on.

Ah, much better. He shined it around the room.

Piles of sleeping bags were everywhere. He shined the light on the windows. Curtains leaned against the window frames like giants. Beyond them, he saw the outline of the porch.

*Nothing to be afraid of*, he told himself.

The sound came again. It sounded like tapping. Was someone at the door?

He felt his muscles freeze. He pointed his flashlight at the door. But the tapping changed places.

Quickly, he shined his flashlight on the wall.

Nothing there.

*Phooey*. He switched the flashlight off. *I'm not scared*, Dunkum told himself.

Then he saw it.

A shadow on the wall! A big black shadow. *How can that be? It's dark*, he thought.

Dunkum felt his heart pounding. Still, he couldn't stop staring.

What *was* it?

He blinked his eyes shut. Then he opened them wide.

The shadow was a raven. The bird was huge. It had a long, scary beak and two skinny legs. And the body—the body was enormous.

It was just like Poe's raven.

Dunkum could hardly swallow. He was too scared to move.

Suddenly, the tapping stopped. The *whooooosh*ing stopped, too. And Dunkum heard only Jason's breathing.

"Hey, Jason," he whispered. "Wake up."

But Jason kept on sleeping. So Dunkum shook him. "There's a raven in the house." He said it louder this time.

Jason popped up. "What?" He rubbed his eyes. "Where's a raven? I don't see anything."

"Look! Over there!" Dunkum pointed to the wall.

"Yikes! You're right!" Jason dove down inside his sleeping bag.

"Hey!" Dunkum leaned over and shook his friend. "You're no help."

Slowly, Jason slid back up. "You're not really scared, are you?" he asked.

"What do *you* think?" Dunkum said. "I'm so scared, I want to go home." He meant it. "I'm gonna ask Miss Hershey to drive me home."

"In the middle of the night?" said Jason.

"Yes, right now!" Dunkum started to push himself out of his sleeping bag. "I'm not staying in this haunted house another minute."

Jason reached over and grabbed Dunkum's arm. "Wait. I have a better idea. Give me your flashlight."

Dunkum handed it over. "Here."

The boys got out of bed. They tiptoed to the window and looked out. It was snowing harder than ever.

"Guess you're stuck here," Jason said. "Looks like a blizzard to me."

Dunkum stared at the snow and frowned. He really wanted to go home!

Jason pulled on the hem of Dunkum's pj top. "Don't step on any bodies," he said, laughing.

"That's not funny," Dunkum said.

Jason turned and looked at the wall. "Whoa! It's gone," he said.

"What's gone?" asked Dunkum.

"Your raven," replied Jason.

Dunkum stared at the wall. The raven *was* gone!

"Maybe you were dreaming," Jason said.

"But you saw it, too," Dunkum reminded him.

"Oh, you're right." Jason started to laugh. "But I'm not half as scared as you."

Dunkum wondered why. His friend was being too brave!

Then . . . something moved. A black lump over in the corner, near the hallway.

Dunkum pointed. "Quick! Shine the flashlight!"

*Hisssss!*

"What's that?" Dunkum asked.

"How should I know?" Jason answered.

Dunkum wanted to run.

# Ten

"**W**ho's there?" Dunkum whispered. "Who's hissing?"

Silence.

"Talk to us!" Jason said.

That's when Dunkum heard a new sound. A cat sound. *Meow.*

It was Milo, Miss Hershey's fat black cat. His eyes looked like gold marbles.

The cat jumped over Eric's sleeping bag. Milo ran out of the living room. As he did, something big and floppy fell over.

Dunkum picked it up and ran to the hallway. There was a night-light near the floor. He held the floppy thing up to the dim light. "Hey, check it out," he said. "Someone brought a stuffed Big Bird to the sleep-over."

Jason started to push up his glasses. But they weren't on his nose. Then he coughed kinda funny.

"Wait a minute! This is *yours*, isn't it?" Dunkum said.

Jason shined the flashlight on his own face. He made a silly look and his voice squeaked. "Can't help that I still like my Big Bird."

"But you were shy about it, weren't you? Isn't that why you wouldn't let Abby tell? Because *she* knew what stuffed animal you'd brought?" Dunkum said.

Jason didn't say anything. Probably because Big Bird was such a babyish stuffed animal to have.

So Dunkum dropped the subject. He wanted to check on something. He hurried to the living room and looked back at the hallway. He squinted at the night-light and got down on his hands and knees.

Yep. It was the right angle for a shadow.

Then he propped up Jason's stuffed animal. "Turn off the flashlight," Dunkum said. "Watch."

The boys stared at the wall.

"The shadow doesn't look like a raven *now*," Dunkum said. "Not at all."

He could hardly believe it. Had he only imagined the big black raven?

"Well, we solved that," Jason said. "But next time, remember what the Bible says about fear."

"What's that?" asked Dunkum.

"When you're afraid, trust in God." Jason talked into the flashlight, like it was a microphone. "Please don't ask me what chapter or verse, though."

"Don't worry. I already know," Dunkum said. "It's in Psalms."

"Cool!" said Jason. "Now let's get some Z's."

"Don't forget your Big Bird," teased Dunkum.

"He's sure a funny-looking raven," Jason said. He headed back to his sleeping bag.

But Dunkum stayed near the window. He watched the blizzard.

*Tap-a-tap tap.*

He wasn't afraid anymore. "It's a tree blowing against the house."

Then Dunkum heard another sound.

*Whooooosh!*

He punched the air with his fist. "'Tis the wind and nothing more,'" he quoted.

"Ps-st! Who are you talking to?" Jason whispered across the room.

"Me, myself, and I," Dunkum replied.

"Just so long as it's not that raven," Jason joked.

Dunkum didn't laugh. He went over and crawled into his sleeping bag. "Thanks for reminding me. I forgot all about trusting God tonight."

Jason tossed his stuffed animal at Dunkum. "Here, maybe this'll help you remember," he said.

Dunkum could feel the skinny legs and the long beak. Why'd he ever think Big Bird was a raven? "Silly me," he said. "This house isn't haunted. Never was."

"Huh?" said Jason.

"Oh, nothing," Dunkum replied. He peeked one eye open and took one more look at the wall.

The night-light in the hall cast a shadow. But it was just a big, blobby shadow. Probably Miss Hershey's sleepy, fat cat. Nothing scary.

He turned over and hugged Jason's Big Bird.

*Zzz!* Jason was already snoring.

"Sweet dreams," Dunkum said and smiled.

What a super sleep-over!

# BOOK 18

# The Great TV Turn-Off

For
Amanda Hoffman,
who pulled the plug
and lived to tell about it!
And . . .
for her brother,
Jeremy,
also a *big* fan
in the Sunflower State.
(We miss you in Colorado!)

# One

Eric Hagel slapped the Sunday paper shut. "No TV for me for one whole week. I'm going cold turkey!" he said.

His mother's eyes fluttered. "*What* did you say?"

"You heard right, Mom. America's TV Turn-Off Week starts tomorrow."

Eric's mom cleared off the breakfast table. "Really? My goodness, what a wonderful idea."

"I can't wait to tell my friends," Eric said.

His mother smiled. "Seven days is a long time. Do you think the Cul-de-Sac Kids will go for it?"

"Well, I'm gonna find out," he said.

■■■

Right after church, an emergency club meeting was held at Dunkum Mifflin's house. Nine club members in all, counting Eric.

Abby Hunter sat in the president's chair—a giant beanbag. "The meeting will come to order," she said. "Any old business?"

Eric shook his head. Dunkum and Jason shook theirs, too. And so did Stacy, Carly, Dee Dee, and Abby's adopted Korean brothers—Shawn and Jimmy Hunter.

"OK, what about new business?" asked Abby.

Eric spoke up. "Did everyone read the morning paper? The part about America turning off the TV?"

The kids just stared at him.

"C'mon! Don't you guys read the paper?" he asked.

Abby smiled. "I saw the article."

"So . . . are you with me?" said Eric. "Do you want to pull the plug?"

"On TV?" asked Jason. "Are you kidding?"

The others looked shocked.

"I think it's a great idea," said Eric. "Just think of all the books you could read."

"Maybe we should have a vote," suggested Abby.

"OK with me," said Eric.

"All in favor of no TV, raise your hands," Abby said.

Eric, Abby, and Dunkum shot their hands up. Then, very slowly, Stacy, Jimmy, and Shawn put theirs up, too. They were looking around, though, as they voted.

"Last chance to vote," Eric piped up. He was saying it for Dee Dee's and Carly's sake. They were slowpoke members.

"OK," whispered Carly. But she wasn't smiling about it.

"All against no TV, raise your hands," Abby said.

"Wait!" Very slowly, Jason's hand went up. "I must be crazy," he muttered.

Abby made the report, too. "The vote is carried. We pull the plug on TV. *All* of us."

Jason groaned.

"Hey, you voted for it," Dunkum scolded. "You can't complain now!"

Eric spoke up. "Let's do something totally cool for TV Turn-Off Week."

Jason Birchall's eyes went crossed. "We're skipping TV for a week. Isn't that cool enough?"

"But wait. I have *another* idea," said Eric.

"Let's hear it," said Abby.

The kids listened.

"I think our parents should turn off the TV, too," Eric said. "No TV for anyone."

Dunkum nodded his head. "It's only fair," he said.

"What a double dabble good idea!" Abby said, smiling.

Carly raised her hand. She was Abby's sister. "What about Mr. Tressler? He's not anyone's parent. Should he do it?"

Jason couldn't sit still. He was up dancing and jiving. "Good thinking, Carly. But Mr. Tressler lives alone. He watches tons of TV, especially at night. Who's gonna get *him* to agree?"

"Maybe older folks shouldn't be in on it," Abby suggested.

Eric thought about that. "We oughta have the whole cul-de-sac. If everyone in the whole country is doing it, why not Blossom Hill Lane?" he said.

"OK with me," Abby said.

"So, who's gonna break it to Mr. Tressler?" Jason asked.

"I will," Eric spoke up.

"Way to go, Eric!" said Dee Dee.

"I'll go along," Abby offered.

"I go, too," Shawn said.

So it was set: Eric, Abby, and Shawn would pay a visit to Mr. Tressler.

"Now, what about our parents?" Eric said. "Can we get *them* to black out the TV?"

"We can try!" Dunkum said.

"What if they won't?" Dee Dee asked. "What then?"

The kids were silent. Their brains were buzzing. Especially Eric's. "I've got it!" he said. "If we catch someone sneaking TV time, we pack up the TV remotes. No questions asked."

"Even grown-ups?" asked little Jimmy. His big brown eyes looked big.

"Especially grown-ups," Eric said.

"Everyone should sign a promise sheet," Dunkum said.

"I'll make up a bunch," Abby offered.

"And I'll help," Stacy said.

Eric grinned. What a terrific plan!

# Two

E ric knocked on the door to his grandpa's bedroom. Grandpa Hagel had lived with them since Eric and his mom had moved from Germany.

"Come in," Grandpa called.

Eric hoped this wouldn't take long. He hoped his grandpa would agree right away.

"Sit down, sit down," Grandpa said. He was propped up in bed.

Eric pulled up a chair. "Is your afternoon nap over?" he asked.

"*Now* it is." Grandpa smiled a sleepy smile.

"Good, 'cause I have a great idea," Eric said. He began to tell about TV Turn-Off Week. "We want the grown-ups on the block to join in."

Grandpa rubbed his chin. "Well, well. That *is* an interesting idea."

Eric waited, holding his breath. What would Grandpa say?

"Where'd you come up with this, young man?"

"It was in the morning paper," Eric said. He felt nervous. Should he tell Grandpa Hagel about the club meeting?

"The newspaper, eh?" Grandpa said.

"I can show it to you," Eric said.

Grandpa waved his hand. "No, no. Don't bother. I've heard of such things. Don't they do this every year?"

Eric said, "Sure do."

"Well, OK. Count me in," said Grandpa.

Yes! Eric was thrilled. "All right!" he hollered.

"Settle down," Grandpa said. "It's not a big deal."

"It *is* a big deal," Eric said. "Thanks, Grandpa!"

Eric went over to the big bed. "Any ideas about Mom? How can I get *her* to give up TV?" he asked.

Grandpa scratched his head. "Well now,

that's gonna be tricky. She loves her exercise shows."

Eric wondered what to do. "Do you think she'll sign the promise sheet?"

"Never hurts to ask," said Grandpa.

"True," said Eric. But he knew his mom might not sign.

In fact, there was a strong chance she'd say no.

■■■

*Brr-i-i-ing!*

Eric hurried to answer the phone.

"Sign-up sheets are ready," Abby said.

"Good! I'll be right over," Eric replied.

"How'd it go with your grandpa?" asked Abby.

"Easy as pie," said Eric. "Now, if I can just get my mom to listen."

"How hard can it be?" Abby said. "She'll want to go along with all the neighbors. Won't she?"

"She'll want to keep up with her exercises, too," Eric told her.

"Oh, I forgot," said Abby. "She's into fitness."

"Well, wish me luck," said Eric.

"How about I *pray* for you," Abby said.

Eric thought that was far better.

"When should we visit Mr. Tressler?" Abby asked.

"Before supper tonight," Eric suggested.

"OK."

"I'll come over right after I talk to my mom," Eric said.

"See you later, alligator," Abby said.

"After a while, crocodile," Eric answered.

"Next time, porcupine," Abby added.

"Not too soon, baboon," Eric replied.

"Okeydoke, artichoke," Abby said.

"Bye-bye, horsefly," Eric finished.

# Three

Eric rang the door at the Hunters' house. Carly and Jimmy came to the door together. They were dressed like Bible characters.

"We're David and Goliath. Wanna see our play?" Carly asked.

Eric smiled. "Maybe later. I have to talk to Abby."

Carly rolled her eyes. "Oh, you came to see *Abby*, did you?"

"Cut the comedy," he said. "Where's your sister?"

Jimmy grinned up at him. "Better watch out," he said. He held up his slingshot. "I come in name of God!"

"That's what David's supposed to tell

*Goliath,*" Eric said. "Here, point your sling-shot at Carly."

"She not Carly Anne Hunter. Now sister is *big* giant!" Jimmy shouted.

Eric had never heard Jimmy talk so loud. But then, Jimmy hadn't heard Bible stories till he came to the United States last Thanksgiving.

"Come in and wait. I'll go get Abby," said Carly, the enemy giant.

Jimmy zipped off after her, holding out his slingshot.

Eric ended up waiting in the kitchen. It was impossible *not* to wander in there. Mrs. Hunter was making chocolate-chip cookies. They were still warm. And the chocolate pieces were all gooey when she gave him one.

"Mm-m, thanks!" Eric said. "My favorite."

"Everybody's favorite," Mrs. Hunter agreed.

Soon, Abby and Shawn came downstairs. They had a bunch of papers. "Here they are," Abby said.

Eric looked at the sign-up sheets. And Shawn ate cookies.

The promise sheet was very cool. It said:

*I promise not to watch TV for one whole week. I will not turn on the TV set from March 2 through March 8. If I am caught sneaking TV, the Cul-de-Sac Kids will box up my TV remote and put it away. On March 8, my remote control will be returned.*

*Signed* _____

"Hey, this is great," Eric said. "How'd you think this up?"

Abby shrugged. "It's nothing much. Anybody could've done it."

"Not *this* body," Eric said and laughed.

Abby reached for a cookie. "This is my third one," she whispered. "Here, have another."

Eric thought she'd never ask. "Thanks," he said.

"Want some milk to go with it?" Abby opened the cupboard for a glass.

"Sure!"

Abby poured milk for Eric. Then for her brother Shawn.

They drank milk and ate warm cookies together. They watched the David and Goliath show. But the story ended too quickly

when Goliath (Carly) turned the slingshot on David (Jimmy).

"That's not how the story goes," Abby said, giggling.

Eric hooted with laughter.

Then Mrs. Hunter tempted the future king of Israel. She did it by bringing out more cookies.

Wicked Goliath spied them. "Time out," she declared. "The play is over."

"Not over!" Little David whined and fussed. He took a handful of cookies. "Time for chocolate manna!"

"That's a *different* story," Eric said.

"Eric's right," said Mrs. Hunter. "You may continue the play tomorrow."

"Yay! We'll do a play instead of watching TV," Abby said. Then she showed her mother the sign-up sheet.

"What's this?" Mrs. Hunter said.

"Take a look," Abby said.

Eric wondered what would happen. He crossed his fingers behind his back. Would Mrs. Hunter promise no TV? Would she sign?

"We want the whole cul-de-sac to agree," Abby said softly. "One hundred percent."

Jimmy wiped his mouth. "Jimmy sign now!"

"Wait a minute," Mrs. Hunter said. She found a pen in her kitchen drawer. "Ladies first." She was smiling.

The kids watched Mrs. Hunter sign her name.

"Cool! You're the first on the block," Eric said.

Mrs. Hunter twirled around the kitchen. The kids clapped and cheered, especially Eric.

After all, it was *his* idea.

Now . . . off to Mr. Tressler's house!

Would the old gentleman want to be cool, too?

# Four

Eric, Abby, and Shawn crossed the street. They headed for Mr. Tressler's house at the end of the cul-de-sac.

"Hide the sign-up sheet," Eric said.

"How come?" asked Abby.

"Mr. Tressler not like?" Shawn asked.

"We should just go for a visit. After we're there awhile, we'll tell him about the TV turn-off," Eric suggested.

"Double dabble good idea," Abby said. She folded the paper and put it in her jacket.

Shawn nodded. "Eric is right."

So they just visited. They talked about Mr. Tressler's doves. But their neighbor wanted to talk about TV.

"Have you watched the Adventure Channel?" he asked.

"Sometimes," Eric said.

"We don't watch TV during supper," Abby said.

"Not good for family talking," Shawn said.

"Well, I'd pay double for it," Mr. Tressler said.

*Gulp!* Eric was worried.

"Did any of you see the dolphin show?" Mr. Tressler asked.

"When?" Eric asked.

Mr. Tressler glanced at the ceiling. He was thinking. "Two nights ago, I believe."

"I see dolphins in a movie," Shawn spoke up. "I see them swim with people."

Mr. Tressler's face lit up. "That's it! That's like the show I saw." He seemed so pleased. He kept talking about the one-hour show.

Eric tried to catch Abby's eye. He made several motions with his hands.

Finally, she looked at him.

Eric pointed to the pocket of her jacket.

Then Abby caught on. She pulled out one of the sign-up sheets.

Eric nodded. *Good!* Now maybe they could

discuss their plan. He was about to bring up the subject. But he stopped.

Mr. Tressler was reaching for the TV remote control.

*What's he doing?* Eric wondered.

"Say, would you like to watch TV with me?" Mr. Tressler glanced at the wall clock. "One of my favorite shows is coming on. How about it?"

Poor Mr. Tressler. He was looking around at each of them. Shawn, Abby, and Eric were silent. They didn't know what to do or say.

At last, Eric spoke up. "OK, we'll watch your show."

Abby's eyes blinked with surprise.

"We'll watch with you. But it could be the *last* one you see. Till next week, that is," Eric said.

"Excuse me?" Mr. Tressler pulled on his bow tie.

Eric crossed the room. He took a sign-up sheet from Abby. "Let me explain."

Mr. Tressler was frowning. "Please do," he said.

"The whole country is turning off the TV," Eric said. "Starting tomorrow."

"And we want the rest of the block to join in," Abby said.

Shawn was nodding. "Cul-de-Sac Kids and grown-ups no watch television one week," he said.

Mr. Tressler gasped. "How will I enjoy my meals? I *always* watch the news during supper."

"What about the radio?" Abby asked. "You could *listen* to the news."

"Great idea!" Eric said.

Mr. Tressler shook his head. "It's not the same."

"Maybe better," Shawn said. "Use more imagination."

Mr. Tressler began to chuckle. "You kids want this badly. I can see that."

Eric nodded his head. "We sure do!"

"Well, I don't know . . ." The old man paused. "It's awfully lonely in this house."

Eric felt sorry for his neighbor. "Why don't you have supper with us? My grandpa will miss TV, too. You'd be good company for each other," he said.

Abby and Shawn were grinning.

Mr. Tressler sighed. "The world might stop

spinning without TV," he said. "Why don't you go ahead? Leave this old man out of it."

"No, Mr. Tressler. We *want* you in on the fun," Abby insisted.

*Fun? Who said it would be fun?* Eric scratched his head. Maybe Mr. Tressler was right. Maybe only certain people should do the turn-off thing.

Going without TV might be boring. What would *Eric* do all week without it?

Seven days was a very long time!

# Five

**E**ric could hardly watch Mr. Tressler's show. The dolphins were fine. But he just kept thinking about next week.

No TV? Was he crazy?

Maybe it was time for another club meeting. An emergency meeting.

But wait. The other Cul-de-Sac Kids might call him a wimp.

He could almost hear little Dee Dee Winters. She'd be giggling herself silly. "You gotta be tough, Eric," she might say. "Can't you read books or play ball or something else?"

He wouldn't be wimpy. He'd made the choice. Everyone else was jumping on board. Except Mr. Tressler. And maybe Eric's own mother.

He looked at his watch. There was a commercial on TV. "I need to talk to my mom," he spoke up.

Mr. Tressler perked up his ears. "Is your mother giving up TV?"

"I haven't asked her yet," Eric answered.

Shawn got up and stretched. "I ready," he said.

"Don't you want to watch the rest?" Mr. Tressler asked.

Abby stood up. "We do, and we don't." She held up the promise sheet. "It's almost dark. We need to talk to some more neighbors."

Mr. Tressler seemed a bit sad. "Don't go away mad," he said.

"Oh, we're not," said Abby. "It's your choice."

"Free country," Shawn piped up.

"You're right about that," Mr. Tressler said. "But thanks for asking anyway."

"Any time," Eric muttered.

*Rats!* How many more people wouldn't sign?

■■■

Eric took two promise sheets into the house. He found his mother in the kitchen warming up leftovers. They always had left-overs for Sunday supper.

"Hey, Mom," he said.

She glanced at him. "What's that?"

He put the sign-up sheet on the counter. "Just something. It's kinda dumb, I guess."

Grandpa came into the room just then. "Why so gloomy?" he asked Eric.

"Things aren't working out," Eric muttered.

"What things?" his mother asked.

Eric told them everything, including about Mr. Tressler's TV habit. "He says he can't eat supper without watching the news."

"That's funny," Grandpa spoke up. "The evening news gives me a stomach pain!"

Eric had to laugh. "Good one, Grandpa. I'll have to try *that* on Mr. Tressler."

"Be my guest," said Grandpa. "The old fella needs a boot in the pants."

"Now, Grandpa!" Eric's mother scolded.

"Excuse me, but it's true. Let's see what I can do," Grandpa said. "First, though, *I* want to sign up for turn-off torture."

Eric laughed out loud.

Grandpa gazed at Eric's mother. "And what about our fair queen?"

Eric's mother shook her head. "I can't go without exercising."

"You could run up and down the cul-de-sac," Eric suggested. "No one'll mind. Right, Grandpa?"

Grandpa nodded cheerfully. "Eric's absolutely right."

"Are *all* the neighbors signing?" Eric's mother asked.

"The kids are asking their parents right now." After all, they didn't have much longer. Tomorrow was the first day.

"Well, OK. I won't be a party pooper." Eric's mother signed her name. "I hope I don't live to regret this." She rubbed her hips.

"You won't," promised Eric. He hoped it was true.

■■■

Eric had to call Abby. "Everyone at *my* house signed," he bragged.

"So did all the Hunter family," Abby said.

"What about Dunkum and Jason? Any problems?" Eric asked.

"They've already called in to report," Abby said. "And Stacy didn't have trouble, either."

"Maybe 'cause her mom works," Eric reminded Abby.

"But after a long day, some people like to veg out in front of the TV," Abby said. "Stacy's mom is a good sport."

Eric knew she was right. "What about Mr. Tressler?" he asked. "Should we just let it go? Let him spoil our block record?"

"Guess so," Abby said. "It's not for a school grade or anything."

Eric was glad it wasn't a test.

They talked a little more. About their pets—Abby's dog and Eric's hamster.

Then he heard a knock. "Someone's at the door."

"See you at school tomorrow," Abby said. "And remember, no TV."

"How can I forget?" he teased.

They hung up, and Eric hurried to the door. There stood Mr. Tressler.

"Well, hello," Eric said. "What are *you* doing here?"

"Let's talk," said the old gentleman.

# Six

"Come in," said Eric. He took his neighbor's coat.

"Thank you," Mr. Tressler said.

Eric led him to the living room. "Have a seat."

Mr. Tressler chose Grandpa's chair. "I've been thinking," he said.

"Yes?"

"Am I the only coward in the cul-de-sac?"

"Coward?" said Eric. "What do you mean?"

The old man stared at his cane. "What I mean is, I want to sign on the dotted line."

"You do?" Eric nearly shouted.

"Where's that promise sheet or whatever?" Mr. Tressler said.

Eric stood up. He glanced out the window. "Don't go away. I'll be right back!"

He dashed out the front door so fast he forgot to put on his coat. He headed across the street to Abby's.

Soon, he was back. "Here's the sign-up sheet. Read it carefully," Eric warned.

Mr. Tressler frowned. "Why's that?"

"Abby's pretty smart. She wrote all this stuff." He pointed out the part about boxing up the TV remotes. "But you shouldn't worry. That won't happen to you."

"Never fear. I'll suffer through," said Mr. T.

Eric grinned. "I'm glad you came over. And don't forget, you can always have supper with us."

"Better talk to your mother about that," Mr. T said.

"She'll call you, OK?"

"Wonderful." The old man seemed happier now.

"Table talk at our house is better than the news anytime." Eric got Mr. Tressler's coat.

"Tell your grandad hello for me."

"Sure will," said Eric. "He's probably upstairs watching TV. Getting his last fix, you know?"

Mr. T waved his cane and gave a wink.

Eric watched the old man walk down the sidewalk.

*Yahoo!*

One hundred percent for Blossom Hill Lane!

He ran upstairs and watched TV with Grandpa. Their last chance.

# Seven

It's Monday, the first day of TV Turn-Off Week," Eric's teacher told the class. "I pulled the plug on my TV. How many of you did, too?"

Eric was proud to raise his hand. He looked around the room. Nearly all the kids had their hands up.

"That's really terrific," said Miss Hershey.

Eric wanted to check out lots of books from the school library today. Abby, Stacy, and Dunkum were going to meet him there. Shawn and Jason had other plans. They were going to ice-skate till their legs hurt.

Going without TV wouldn't be easy. Anybody knew that.

And it *wasn't* easy.

It was horrible.

■■■

After school, Eric kept staring at the black TV. It was turned off, of course. But he looked at it anyway. Even his stack of books didn't help.

"What a nightmare," he muttered.

Eric went upstairs. On the way, he passed Grandpa's room. The small TV seemed to stare at *him*. He turned his head away.

"That you, Eric?" Grandpa called.

Eric peeked into the room, trying not to look at the dark TV. "Hi, Grandpa," he said.

Grandpa tilted his head and chuckled. "Something the matter?"

"Oh, nothing," Eric said. But his eyes were drawn to the silent one-eyed monster!

Suddenly, Grandpa reached for the TV remote.

"No! Don't do that!" Eric shouted.

Grandpa dropped the remote on his bed. "Gotcha!"

"Aw, don't scare me," pleaded Eric. "I thought you forgot already."

Grandpa shook his head. "I made a promise. I'll keep it."

Eric eyed the remote. "Maybe you'd better put that away."

"Good thinking," he said. "Here."

Eric put the remote high in the closet. "Don't forget where it is," he said.

Grandpa reached for a bag of jelly beans. "Any ideas?"

"For what?"

"For keeping my brain busy," said Grandpa.

"I've got a bunch of books," Eric told him.

Grandpa grinned. "Good choice. Let's read one together. Maybe we can discuss it later."

It sounded almost like school to Eric. But he would give it a try. "What's your favorite?" he asked.

"Got a good mystery?" Grandpa asked.

"I'll check." Eric went back downstairs. He found an adventure mystery. "We need some popcorn, too," he said to himself.

His mother was chopping cabbage in the kitchen. "Hi, Eric. How's cold turkey going?"

He shook his head. "So far, it's horrible. I think Grandpa's fading fast," he said. "What about you? Did you exercise?"

She nodded. "I ran around the cul-de-sac six times."

"Really?"

"The neighbors must think I'm nuts," she said.

"How come?" asked Eric.

"Well, Mr. Tressler came outside. He asked if I was all right." She laughed.

"What did you tell him?" Eric asked.

"I said I was in withdrawal," she replied.

Eric understood. "Then what?"

"Mr. Tressler stayed outside, too. He walked around his driveway," she said. "And every time I came around the corner, he'd wave."

"It's about time Mr. T got some fresh air." Eric was glad. The Great TV Turn-Off was doing *somebody* some good.

"I invited him for supper tomorrow night," his mother said.

"That'll be cool," said Eric. "I like Mr. Tressler." He almost forgot why he'd come to the kitchen.

Then his mother said, "Want some popcorn?"

"How'd you know?" he said.

"You have that look," she said.

Eric grinned. "Thanks, Mom."

Just then, they heard thumps overhead.

"Sounds like Grandpa dropped a shoe," Eric said.

"Probably on purpose," his mother said. "Better get back upstairs. I'll bring the popcorn."

Eric closed his eyes as he passed the living room. He felt his way to the stairs.

Why did the TV keep pulling him, anyway?

# Eight

Tuesday was the second day of TV Turn-Off.

Pure misery.

All of Eric's favorite after-school specials were on. But he'd promised he wouldn't watch them.

Everyone else was stuck, too. "All across the country," he reminded himself. "Everybody's bored like me."

Grandpa came downstairs for tea. First time in a long time. "Where's that mystery book of yours?" he asked.

Eric found it. "Here you go," he said.

Grandpa settled into his favorite chair. "Now, where were we?" And he began to read.

Eric enjoyed hearing Grandpa. Sometimes

he would change his voice around. It made the characters almost real.

By suppertime, Grandpa had to stop. "Help your mother set the table," he said.

Eric wanted to know what happened. "Can we read after supper?"

"Only if you read to *me*," Grandpa said.

"It's a deal!"

■■■

Mr. Tressler showed up on time for supper. He was dressed up in a nice coat and suspenders. The works.

"Welcome, neighbor," Grandpa said.

Eric held the door open. He was glad to do it. Having their neighbor come for a meal was a great idea. It might keep Mr. T from sneaking TV.

"Whatcha been doing?" Eric asked him.

"I've got a lot of time on my hands," Mr. Tressler answered. "Don't really know what to do with myself."

"I know what you mean," Eric agreed.

Grandpa waved them into the living room. "Let's chat by the fire," he said.

Eric's mother offered some hot tea.

"Thank you, don't mind if I do," said Mr. T.

Grandpa struck up a conversation. He and Mr. T talked about their favorite birds. Doves, canaries, and parakeets. They laughed every so often as they all sipped tea, even Eric.

Eric couldn't remember listening to two old men chatter. It was kinda fun. And for several minutes he forgot that he missed TV!

After supper, his mother brought out some games. "Anybody interested in playing Monopoly?" she asked.

Mr. Tressler's eyes lit up. "I used to play that game as a teenager. It's been a long, long time."

Grandpa was ready to take on Mr. T. He seemed eager to shuffle the cards.

Eric got excited, too. "Are you gonna play?" he asked his mother.

She pulled out a chair. "Count me in!"

They played till Eric's bedtime. The mantel clock struck nine times.

"Wow, I can't believe it!" he said.

Mr. Tressler scooted his chair back. "Time flies when you're having fun."

"You can say that again!" Grandpa answered.

Eric piped up. "Time flies when you're—"

"Enough!" His mother laughed.

"Sorry, Mom," he said.

They were all grinning at him now.

"Thanks for a great evening," Mr. T said.

"Any time," Grandpa said.

"How about my place next time?" Mr. T offered.

Eric's mother smiled. "We'd love to come."

"Can you cook?" Eric asked.

Mr. Tressler laughed out loud. "You'll have to judge that for yourself, young man."

They said their good-byes.

Before Eric went to bed, he hugged his mom. "I didn't miss the TV all night," he whispered.

She kissed his head. "Me neither."

Eric could hardly wait to see the other Cul-de-Sac Kids. How were his friends doing without TV time?

# Nine

**W**ednesday morning was crazy.

Eric got up early for his paper route. He felt tired. He'd gone to bed late. But playing Monopoly last night was worth it.

He bundled up to go outdoors. It was snowing softly.

First stop, Mr. Tressler's house.

Usually he heard flute music this early. Mr. T liked to practice before sunrise. It was his special thing.

Eric tossed the paper onto the porch.

*Phlat!* It bounced off the railing.

"I can do better than that." He went to find the paper. Then he carried it up onto the porch.

That's when he heard something. It sounded

like the voice of a news reporter. He didn't want to snoop. But he was curious.

Eric took a quick peek. Through the door window, he saw a flashing light.

"Oh no!" he said. "Mr. T's in trouble now!"

Sure enough. The TV in the living room was on.

He wondered what to do.

Eric took another peek. *This* time he saw Mr. T lying on the sofa. Sound asleep.

■■■

At school, Eric told his friends what he'd seen.

"Maybe his TV came on by itself," Jason said, laughing.

"TVs don't do that," Eric argued.

Abby nodded. "Eric's right."

"Eric's *always* right," Dee Dee piped up. "I'm sick of it!" She ran to the merry-go-round.

"What's wrong with her?" Eric said.

"She's a little freaked out. We *all* are," Carly said. "Giving up TV is a big deal."

Abby shook her head. "But a promise is a promise."

"Rules are rules," said Dunkum.

Eric agreed. "Mr. T loses his remote control."

"First thing after school," Jason said.

"Poor Mr. Tressler," Stacy said. "Do we *really* have to box it up?"

Abby reminded her of the promise sheet. "We all signed it. Remember?"

"What if Mr. T just forgot?" asked Dunkum.

Jason squeezed into the circle. "Maybe his TV got lonely."

Nobody paid attention.

"Has anyone *almost* turned on their TV?" Eric asked.

Shawn and Jimmy looked at each other. "I not," said Jimmy. "I see Shawn, though."

Eric perked up his ears. "Surely not Shawn," he said.

Shawn nodded his head. "I come very close." It sounded like *velly* close.

Abby twisted her hair. "Maybe we should have lots of club meetings this week," she said. "To keep us out of trouble."

"Good idea," Stacy said. "Let's meet at my house after school."

"First we have to visit Mr. Tressler," Eric said.

"That's true," Abby said. "Who's coming along?"

Nobody blinked an eye.

Eric looked at Abby. "I guess it's you and me."

Abby looked around. "Well, that's settled. Eric and I are stuck with the dirty work."

"Spread the word at morning recess," Eric said. "We'll have a club meeting at Stacy's."

"Jimmy and I could put on a play," Carly suggested.

Abby grinned. "David kills Goliath, right?"

"Or the other way around," Carly said.

The school bell rang.

"Bye!" they all called to one another.

Eric ran to the outside door. He was worried and felt funny. Promise sheet or not.

Was it right to take away an old man's remote control?

# Ten

**E**ric rang Mr. Tressler's doorbell. "Are you nervous?" he asked Abby.

"A little," she said.

"Who should do the talking?" he asked.

"You can," she said.

That's when the door opened.

"Good afternoon, Mr. Tressler," they said.

"Hello there, kids," he said. "Come in."

Eric glanced at the TV. *Good*, he thought. *It's off.*

"What can I do for you?" Mr. Tressler asked.

Eric got straight to the point. "Your TV was turned on this morning."

"Oh?" Mr. Tressler said.

"Yes, I was delivering your newspaper. That's when I heard it," Eric said.

Mr. T frowned. "That's funny. I don't remember."

"You don't?" Eric was puzzled.

"Not at all." The old man pulled on his ear. "That's very strange."

Eric looked at Abby. She shrugged back at him. She didn't seem to know what to say, either.

"I saw something else," Eric spoke up. "You were asleep on your couch."

Mr. Tressler looked surprised. "Oh, that's right. I fell asleep there. But I never turned on the TV."

"How could it turn itself on?" Eric knew it sounded ridiculous. "Could you have bumped the remote?"

"Well, I don't know," replied Mr. T. He got up and walked the length of the room. He seemed to be thinking very hard.

"Are you okay?" Abby asked.

"Fine and dandy," he replied. "Now, just a minute. It's coming back to me."

Eric waited. So did Abby.

"I woke up late last night. Needed some warm milk," Mr. T explained. "I was a little under the weather. So I stayed downstairs on the couch. I must have fallen asleep."

Eric wanted to hear how the TV got turned on.

"Yes, I remember now," said Mr. T. "When I awakened this morning, the TV was going. And I was lying on the couch."

Eric and Abby stared at each other. They still didn't know what to say.

"I turned it off right away," Mr. Tressler told them.

Eric scratched his head. He got up and stood at the window. He thought everything over. "Do you ever talk in your sleep?" he asked.

"Don't know that I do" came the reply.

"Have you ever walked in your sleep?" Eric asked.

"How would I know?" Mr. T chuckled. "But you know, it's possible . . ." He paused.

*What?* Eric wondered. *What's he going to say?*

Eric waited, dying to know.

Mr. Tressler sighed. "I may have turned on the TV in my sleep. Out of pure habit." He looked at Eric and Abby. "If so, I'm truly sorry."

Eric felt sorry, too. "I guess we could give you a second chance," he said.

Mr. Tressler shook his head. "Oh no! We play by the rules around here. I signed that sheet of yours. So that's that!"

■■■

Eric felt odd. He didn't want to follow through with this. Not when Mr. T had been asleep!

"It doesn't seem fair," he said.

Abby held the box. "Mr. Tressler's a good sport," she said.

"I insist," said the old man. Then he motioned them into the kitchen. "There's another little TV out here."

Eric couldn't believe it. Mr. Tressler was going to make them box up *both* his TV remotes!

When the boxes were sealed and next to the door, Mr. Tressler smiled. "It's fun living on this street," he said. "You Cul-de-Sac Kids are great."

Abby gave Mr. Tressler a hug. "Only four days to go," she whispered. "Will you be all right?"

"Absolutely," Mr. T replied. "I'll play my flute more. Maybe even at night!"

They laughed with him.

Eric shook his neighbor's hand. "Sorry about all this," he said.

"No need," said Mr. T. "I got what was coming to me."

Eric and Abby said good-bye and walked home. "Guess we oughta think things over next year," Eric said.

"I know what you mean," Abby said. "That was tough."

"Sure was," said Eric.

# Eleven

Eric met Jason at Eric's front door. "What's up?" Eric asked.

"We have to talk," Jason said.

"What about?" Eric said.

"The Great TV Turn-Off idea," Jason said. "It's . . . it's, uh—"

"If you don't like it, say so," Eric said. He was sure Jason was having a hard time. His friend was probably bored silly.

"Listen, you were right about blacking out the TV," Jason said. "I can't believe how good I feel."

Eric could hardly believe his ears!

"I have gobs more time to do stuff. I've started building Lego projects again," he

said. "My parents and I have time to talk to one another."

"Cool," said Eric.

Jason's face looked like Christmas morning. "I'm glad you got us to turn off the TV, Eric," said Jason. "It was the best idea you've ever had."

Eric told him about eating supper with Mr. Tressler. He told about playing games and reading books out loud. "And Mr. Tressler's gonna cook us supper," he said. "Unreal, huh?"

"Wow, that's cool!" replied Jason.

"Very cool," said Eric. "And we're only through the first part of the week. Just think what good friends we're all gonna be!"

Jason pushed up his glasses. He clicked his fingers. "Hey, I've got an idea. Let's turn off the TV forever!"

"Get real," Eric said.

"I'm *serious*! So . . . what do you think?" Jason was pushing it.

"Better wait till the end of this week. We should have a club meeting about it," Eric said.

"Cool!" Jason dashed out the door.

"See you," Eric called.

His mother was doing sit-ups in the kitchen. "How was your day?" she asked.

"Better than ever." He told her about Mr. Tressler's two TVs. "He made us box up both of his remotes."

His mother stopped her exercises. "That's amazing."

"I think I got something started," he explained. "Something Abby might call 'double dabble good.'"

His mother did a thumbs-up. "That's my boy."

Eric grinned. He was dying for his mystery book. And to hear his grandpa's many different reading voices.

He walked past the living room. Didn't even close his eyes this time.

Nope.

The TV didn't stare back at him or call to him. Didn't even pull at him.

Not one bit!

## About the Author

Beverly Lewis thinks all the Cul-de-Sac Kids are super fun. She clearly remembers growing up on Ruby Street in her Pennsylvania hometown. She and her younger sister, Barbara, played with the same group of friends year after year. Some of those childhood friends appear in her Cul-de-Sac Kids series—disguised, of course!

Now Beverly lives with her husband, David, in Colorado, where she enjoys writing books for all ages. Beverly loves to tell stories, but because the Cul-de-Sac Kids series is for children, it will always have a special place in her heart.

Learn more about Beverly and her books at www.beverlylewis.com.